Sunshine and Grimm

Melissa Hosack

WP

Whimsical Publications, LLC

Florida

Sunshine and Grimm is a work of fiction. Names, characters, and incidents are the products of the author's imagination and are either fictitious or are used fictitiously. Any resemblance to actual events or persons, living or dead, is entirely coincidental.

To purchase the authorized electronic edition of *Sunshine and Grimm*, visit www.whimsicalpublications.com

Cover art by Traci Markou
Editing by Brieanna Robertson

ISBN-13: 978-1-940707-22-8

Published in the United States by
Whimsical Publications, LLC
Florida

She'd ordered two vodkas, sliding one to him along the short distance of bar that separated them. "Brings back memories, huh?" She rolled her eyes with a chuckle. "Or maybe in your case, it doesn't." She shrugged in amusement as she swirled the contents around in her glass. "Drink up," she said with a wink. "I doubt it can result in anything weirder than last time."

"I sure hope not," Alex grunted with a voice low and gravely.

They'd both downed their drinks together and slammed the empty glasses back down to the bar simultaneously.

He'd felt the liquid burn its way down his throat. It was like drinking liquid sunlight. "I hate vodka," he'd complained with a grimace.

With her face flushed from the alcohol, Lacy agreed. After that, they decided to stay away from the vodka. It made them do crazy things.

Lacy had turned to him and asked him to take her out on the dance floor.

Before he could even begin to protest, he'd been grabbed from behind and thrown with inhuman strength toward the dance floor.

That is where he was now, staring up at the ceiling of the Nocturnal Lady and wincing at the pain shooting up his spine from hitting the unforgiving tile. With a groan, he hefted himself off the ground to face his attacker. He saw Lacy's blue eyes widen in surprise, but didn't have time to reassure her that he was perfectly fine before a boot was kicked into his gut. He stumbled backwards onto the dance floor, but finally managed to get a good look at his attacker.

The fangs protruding from the man's mouth were a dead giveaway that he was a vampire. His shirt was a ghastly orange and brown swirl of a mess that reminded Alex of vomit. His pants were brown corduroy with belled bottoms.

"A vampire trapped in the seventies," Alex observed dryly. "Not cool."

Lacy, who had raced to the edge of the dance floor during his attack, giggled at this, seemingly recovered from her initial shock.

He frowned in response. He'd been spending too much time with this little vixen. When had he ever even noticed an enemy's outfit before, let alone commented on it? He didn't do witty banter. He fought. He killed. He went about his day.

While he was distracted by these thoughts, the vampire in 70s apparel aimed a kick at his ribs.

Alex jumped to the side. He avoided the majority of the blow, the vampire's heeled boot grazing his midsection.

Lacy watched with interest as he ducked a punch aimed at his jaw. "You need help, baby?"

Alex yanked a stake from his back pocket, flipping it so the thick end rested in his palm. When the other man charged him, Alex took him by surprise by jamming the stake deep into the vampire's chest. He watched the vampire turn to dust with grim satisfaction, then spun to Lacy. "No. I don't need help. Like you would know what to do with a vampire."

Lacy shrugged, unconcerned.

Alex sighed, but couldn't stop his lip from twitching in amusement as it threatened a smile. "Thank you anyway." He glanced around them. Seeing at least two more vampires approaching, he quickly returned his gaze to her. "I've gotten their attention. Things are probably about to get very violent," he hollered to her over the still pumping music. "You should get somewhere safe."

Lacy nodded. "I absolutely agree. Somewhere safe."

To his amazement, she took five steps away from him and struck a sexy pose. Her foot started tapping, and then her head started bobbing. A moment later, her hips started swaying.

His jaw dropped in disbelief as she started dancing, her body gyrating to the music that pounded through the speakers that surrounded the room. "Lacy," he chastised, "I said somewhere safe!"

She gave him a playful wink and turned her back on him. Her hands lifted above her head, her fists pumping the air in time to the beat of a song he'd never heard before.

"I cannot believe—" Alex's complaints were cut short by a fist colliding with his nose. He grunted in pain, his hand moving to cover his bleeding face as he reeled backwards. "Damn it," he growled. "That wasn't fair." A stupid comment, he knew. Criminals never played fair, and vampires were even worse than humans.

Acknowledgements

I would like to thank all of my readers! The constant support has been amazing. You guys are awesome! Of course, I also have to thank my family. They put up with my obsessive hours in front of the computer and the fact that my mind is often in la-la land where vampires and werewolves are a normal occurrence. And I cannot forget the astounding people at Whimsical. Thank you for saying 'yes' to my stories and helping me bring them to life.

Prologue

Alex Grimm stood in the bathroom doorway of his hotel room feeling cold inside. He'd stopped short upon entering when his eyes landed on the dead body lying grotesquely in his bathtub.

His surprise visitor was in her late thirties. She was beautiful, if one could ignore the dark circles under her eyes left behind by lack of sleep over the past couple days. Her wet, glossy brown hair clung to a cream-colored throat unmarred by her demise. One of her trim legs was thrown over the rim of the tub. She was in perfect health besides, of course, being dead.

Even worse than stumbling upon the deceased by surprise was the disheartening realization that he knew the person. The body in front of him belonged to that of his client, Darlie Smith. She'd come to him for protection, and he'd let her down.

Alex stared at the pale hand draped over the edge of the large tub. Blood trailed down her fingertips to drip onto the floor. Each time a drop of blood hit the tile, he cringed.

The scene was made out to look like a suicide. Darlie's wrists were slashed. The left one was bleeding into the tub, turning the water a rose petal pink. To the Las Vegas Metropolitan Police Department., it would be an open and shut case. Girl throws away her life savings in Vegas and takes the coward's way out. To Alex, it wasn't so simple.

Darlie had come to him because she'd gotten in over her head. Vegas and loan sharks were dangerous to begin with. Add the supernatural to that, and it was a living nightmare.

Alex gave a derisive snort. Vampire loan sharks in Vegas.

It was ridiculous.

If someone these supernatural thugs had lent money to didn't pay up in a timely fashion, they didn't break their kneecaps like a normal Neanderthal. They loaned money in exchange for rough sex and blood from those who didn't pay up. Sometimes, like with Darlie, things went a little too far. They drained a person of blood, leaving just enough to make it look like suicide. No one was going to look too closely at a few extra suicides in a place like Vegas, and they knew it.

He'd dealt with this group of vampires before. For a reasonable fee, he'd been able to help his clients get away, even if it meant killing a few bloodsuckers. The vampires he murdered were always low on the totem pole, so the retaliations were always few if any. This time, things hadn't gone as smoothly as in the past.

Darlie had owed them a mere five thousand dollars. She'd paid them back every cent, but not before her deadline. They'd come after her anyway, looking for a late night snack to appease their blood lust. She'd forfeited her life for a fun weekend.

Alex backed out of the bathroom, feeling sick. Though he was a vampire himself, Darlie's blood held no appeal to him. It didn't smell like a meal. It smelled like defeat. She'd been human. There was no way she could have realized the repercussions of being a couple hours late in payment until it was too late. Upon realizing what she was up against, she'd somehow managed to track him down through word of mouth from others. She then begged for his help, for his protection from other monsters like himself. It had been his job to keep her safe, and he'd failed.

His shoulders slumping in defeat, Alex pulled his cell phone out of his coat pocket and dialed the police department. He would leave an anonymous tip. The room was booked to Darlie, so the authorities wouldn't be able to trace anything back to him.

He would call this in, and then he was going to get really, really drunk. He wanted to forget the sight in the next room, at least for the evening. When the sun set in Vegas the next night, he was going to hunt down every last person involved with the group responsible for Darlie's death, and then he was going to kill them.

Chapter One

Consciousness slowly began returning to Alex. He felt a soft comforter beneath his back and couldn't for the life of him figure out where he was. It couldn't be his hotel room. Darlie was floating in his bathtub, and the entire floor was bound to be swarming with cops by this point.

He quickly ran through his memories of the night before, trying to come up with a good explanation for his current whereabouts. He remembered Darlie, dead. He then remembered the bottom of a shot glass. Anything after that was hazy.

Uncharacteristically, he'd drank. He'd drank and drank and drank. He'd drank until he couldn't remember the image of Darlie. He'd blocked out his failure, forgotten the loss of life. Now, he couldn't remember *anything*.

"Rise and shine!" a perky voice chirped, interrupting his thoughts as they grasped for any semblance of recollection.

Alex heard the unmistakable sound of heavy drapes being tossed aside. An instant later, agony invaded his senses as sunlight splashed across his bare chest. With an involuntary hiss, he rolled off the bed and hid behind the thick mattress, crouching in a defensive stance. "For the love of God," he growled. "Close the blinds!" He heard the mysterious woman sigh, and a moment later, the curtains slid back into place, leaving the room in dark shadows.

"Still on the vampire shtick, I see," the woman commented. "I thought you were just being kinky last night, but apparently, you're fully dedicated to this gimmick."

Alex sucked in a sharp breath of surprise at her vampire

remark. He'd never in his life told anyone his secret. What exactly had he gotten himself into last night? Almost fearfully, he inched upward to see who was talking to him, revealing his head slowly to his unexpected companion.

A woman in her mid-twenties stood staring at him with an amused smirk on her lips. She had blonde hair cut short, brushing along her neck just below her chin. She had a long, beautiful throat. A small bruise accompanied by two nearly microscopic puncture wounds marred her creamy skin. Vampire marks.

Alex had a flash of recollection, of his fangs sliding into her throat like a knife through warm butter. He gave a soft moan of pleasure at the memory before catching himself.

He frowned. This wasn't like him. He didn't hook up with women. He took his blood from animals or donations to blood banks. It had been a long time since he'd taken fresh human blood.

The girl laughed in amusement at the confused expression on his face, swaying almost dance-like on her feet.

This brought his attention away from her neck and to the rest of her body.

She was wearing a pink, lace nightie that left little to the imagination. He could see the shape of her breasts through the sheer fabric and idly wondered when he'd last seen a woman's breasts. One thing he knew for sure, the women he'd last encountered hadn't been dressing nearly as sexy as the modern one in front of him.

Swallowing nervously, he couldn't help his eyes from continuing their perusal of the woman who was inexplicably in the room with him.

Her pants were nowhere to be found. She was wearing only a pair of tiny pink panties that matched her nightgown. Her legs were long and slim, seeming to go on forever.

Alex had a flash of those legs wrapped around his hips, of her breath hot on his neck. The mental image nearly knocked him over. He tightened his grip on the mattress, trying to get the graphic image out of his mind.

In a move girlier than anything he'd ever seen in his life, she skipped to the bed and hopped on. "You are too crazy, Grimm!" she said with a laugh. Grabbing the dark brown hair at the back of his neck, she pulled him toward her.

Before he could even realize what she was doing, her mouth was on his. She kissed him with a fiery passion and familiarity that confused him. Exactly what the hell had gone on last night?

Her fingers slid through the short, dark spikes of his hair as she pulled back only far enough to whisper against his lips. "I want you to do that thing to me again. You know, the thing you did last night."

Alex was mesmerized by her lips, by the taste of her as she moved sensually against him. His confused mind finally won over his hormones, and he asked, "Huh?"

The woman sighed, her breath hot against his mouth. Then she sat back. "You're right," she agreed, though he hadn't suggested anything. "I should get a shower first." She bounced on her knees for a moment before hopping off the bed. "Once we're ready, do you want to head downstairs and hit the slots for a little? Ooh! Or how about a movie? There's this new romantic comedy I'm just dying to see." She lifted her nightgown over her head and let it flutter to the floor as she strode out of the room.

Alex was frozen, kneeling behind the bed in shock. This woman was a whirlwind of energy that left him bewildered.

He was still trying to collect his wits when he heard the shower turn on. His first instinct was to run. He knew he should high-tail it out of there as quickly as he possibly could, but she intrigued him. It was obvious he'd bitten this woman. After so long, why would he slip up like this?

Slowly, he climbed to his feet. Giving the curtains a wary glance, he inched toward the bathroom. As he moved, he wracked his brain for this captivating woman's name. Surely she'd told him.

His hazy memory was telling him something with an 'L'. "Laney, Lucy, Lexy?" he asked himself quietly. Settling on a name, he tapped on the open bathroom door. "Lexy?" he called out.

The glass door to the shower slid open with a bang. The blonde inside stood dripping, hands on her naked hips. "Lexy?" she snarled in outrage. "I'm not your fucking car. My name is Lacy. You of all people should know that."

Alex didn't drive a Lexus, but he wasn't about to correct her. He went to apologize for not knowing her name, but was distracted by her breasts. Soap was trailing down them, leaving behind bubbles that he had the sudden, desperate urge to lick away.

Alex blinked and took a step back, surprised by his reaction. Though he supposed he couldn't exactly blame himself. Last night notwithstanding, it had been a long time since he'd seen a naked woman. A really long time. "I...I'm sorry. Lacy is a very pretty name."

She shrugged, but a small smile touched her lips at his compliment. "Thanks. My friends call me Sunshine, though, seeing as how I'm so bubbly."

Alex flinched. The irony was not lost on him. He was a vampire who'd just hooked up with a girl nicknamed Sunshine. "I think I'll stick with Lacy."

She shrugged again, all annoyance disappearing from her face. "I can't really be surprised that your memory is a bit hazy. You were totally wasted last night. I've never seen someone consume that much alcohol in one evening. A normal person would be dead after that much vodka. Not you, though," she said with a wink as she ducked back into the shower. "You're special."

"I hate vodka," Alex murmured almost to himself.

She'd left the shower door open, so she examined him as she lathered shampoo into her hair. At his comment, she made a scoffing noise. "Could have fooled me."

"I don't drink." He felt the need to argue, though the only part of last night after discovering Darlie he clearly remembered was downing shots. He wasn't inherently against drinking. It was just that alcohol didn't have the same effect on vampires as it did humans. It took a whole hell of a lot of alcohol to get a vampire drunk. Seeing as he needed a level head for his job, he didn't much see the point of drinking.

Lacy let out a delighted laugh at his denial. "Next you'll say you don't have amazing sex either."

Alex frowned as she turned off the shower. "I *don't* have amazing sex. Ever."

"I'm going to pretend I didn't hear that and not take offense," she responded casually as she motioned behind him. "Hand me a towel."

Absentmindedly, he grabbed a towel from the rack and held it out to her.

Instead of taking the towel from him, Lacy stepped into his chest. She wrapped his arms around her, cocooning her body in the big towel and his embrace.

Alex jumped in surprise when she leaned close and nuzzled his throat. He was torn between pushing her away and pulling her closer.

"Mmm," she mumbled. "The cologne you wear is intoxicating. It makes me want to...well, you saw last night what it makes me want to do."

He frowned at the top of her head. "I don't—"

"Yeah, yeah," she cut him off. "You don't wear cologne." Pulling away, she gave him a swift smack across the butt of his sweatpants. "Hit the showers, sexy." With that, she sauntered out of the room.

Alex stood without moving for a moment, stunned by the events of the morning. This woman didn't seem to be ready to bolt. She wasn't screaming in fear. It wasn't the usual reaction he received from women. He wasn't used to socializing, to speaking to anyone who wasn't a client. Humans, people in general for that matter, didn't like him. He wasn't fun. He lived for his work, and that tended to bore mostly everyone.

Lacy was definitely misguided about his personality. He almost hated that he would have to inform her that there wasn't a single sexy, let alone interesting, thing about him.

As he brooded over this, Alex stepped out of his sweats and set them carefully aside. Without even realizing what he was doing, he followed Lacy's orders. He was in the shower cleaning shampoo from his hair before it dawned on him.

He shrugged it off. He supposed it didn't matter. He needed a shower anyway, and this gave him time to think, time to decide what to do with the overly energetic blonde in the next room.

Putting his face under the spray of water, he let out a whooshing breath. Sure. It wasn't necessary for him to breathe anymore, but it helped him think, helped him clear his head. He was going to need a clear mind to deal with the complications he'd created in his complication-free life.

At that thought, the shower door flew open.

Alex spun toward the intruder with an instinctual snarl. His fangs were bared, and he was prepared to strike at the first sign of an attack.

It was Lacy's unconcerned expression that greeted him. "Ooh, scary," she said with a giggle, her tone mocking.

It took him a moment to see her through the water dripping into his eyes and another moment to lower his hackles. It was instinct for him to fight, to protect himself. He'd spent hundreds of years teaching his body to automatically be on defense. He couldn't just shut it off. Not even for a smoking hot, unthreatening woman.

The woman in question had lost the towel and was now parading around in a skimpy pair of panties and matching blood red bra.

He felt a pang of longing in his fangs as he stared at her slender, exposed neck. "What do you want?" he finally managed to get out, though somewhat breathlessly.

"I just wanted to see what the plans were for today. You never did answer me on that." She leaned against the wall and stared at him with a wicked grin. "Plus, I wanted to get a look at you in your naked glory when I wasn't so tipsy."

At that, Alex quickly turned off the shower and motioned behind her at the towels. "I have to work," he said stiffly.

She pouted as she reached for one of the towels. "You have to work?" she asked in disappointment. "In Vegas?" Her expression pinched in silent disapproval. "You work at one of the casinos?"

His expression turned just as disapproving as hers. "No," he said in a clipped tone. "I do not work in a casino. I am a private detective specializing in the supernatural."

"Ooh," Lacy cooed, thrusting a towel at him. "A private detective. That's sexy! Much better than a casino worker." She returned to her spot against the wall. "Not that there's anything wrong with working in a casino. I just expected something more exotic from a vampire," she teased.

Alex edged around her to get back into the bedroom. "Well, like I said, I have work to do, so..." He caught sight of his black, leather duffel bag and lifted it off the floor. He then tossed it to the bed and yanked it open.

At that instant, Lacy hopped onto the bed. She bounced on her knees in excitement. "So what are we going to do? Hunt down evil vampires? Can I go undercover? I'd be a good spy. People like me. They talk to me, tell me things."

He tried very hard not to stare at her breasts as she

bounced up and down. Tightening his grip on the towel around his waist, he cleared his throat. "Um...I think you are confused. *I* will be working. You will be doing whatever it is you would normally do on a day such as today."

"There is nothing normal about today," she countered. Leaping off the bed, she sauntered toward her open suitcase, which was resting on the dresser.

It looked as if there had been an explosion. Panties and shirts and God only knew what else were everywhere. Alex actually shuddered at the disorganization.

"You aren't running off without me," she informed him. "It's impolite. Besides, I want to see what my new husband does for a living."

Alex flinched at her statement. Surely she hadn't just said what he thought he'd heard. He could have sworn she'd said husband. Turning to face her, he nervously asked, "What did you just say?"

"I said I wanted to see what my new husband does for a living," Lacy repeated as she stepped into a tiny miniskirt. "Did I say that wrong?" she inquired as she fastened the button on the skirt. "Should it be *I want to see what my new husband does for his unliving*? Is that more accurate?"

"We're married?" Alex asked breathlessly as she pulled a bright pink t-shirt over her head. "How? When?" In his mind, he added, *More importantly, why*?

Lacy laughed and raced over to him. She hopped up into his arms and wrapped her legs around his waist, nearly pulling his towel off.

He stumbled backwards and barely managed to keep his balance. He supported her out of instinct, pressing his hands to her thighs to keep her from falling off of him, or worse, dragging him to the floor.

She kissed him, her lips soft and warm, alive. "Last night," she breathed against his lips. "It was amazing. You really know how to make a girl feel special."

He gave her a look of skepticism. "Really?" he asked. "Are you sure we're talking about the same person?"

Lacy slid down his body until her feet touched the floor. "Yes." She slapped his chest playfully. "You're so funny."

"I'm not—" Alex went to protest, but froze when she pulled back to walk away from him and he caught sight of something on her hand. He swiftly grabbed her wrist and yanked her back toward him.

"Ooh, are you getting kinky?" she asked, eyes lighting with interest.

"No," he said dryly. He lifted her hand so he could get a better look. "You're wearing my ring. It's the family crest. It's been passed down for—"

"For centuries and centuries," she finished. "Your mom used it as a wedding band. You told me this already."

Alex's fingers instinctively tightened on her wrist, not letting her move the ring out of his line of sight even if it made him appear threatening. "Why are you wearing it?" he asked through clenched teeth. "This ring holds sentimental value for me. I never take it off."

Though he held her tightly, Lacy gave him an affectionate smile that could melt even the coldest heart. "All the more reason to give it to me. You will cherish and keep me as close to you as you've done with this ring in the past...or so you said last night during your vows."

Alex felt his anger melt away at her comment and the innocent look in her sparkling blue eyes. "That was very romantic of me," he said skeptically.

"Very," Lacy purred in agreement. She moved in close and pressed her lips to his. "You're probably the most romantic man I've ever met." She kissed him again, deepening this one and pressing her body against his.

To his surprise, after a moment's hesitation, Alex returned her kiss. His mouth was stiff against hers, but he felt himself relaxing, felt his lips going soft. He slid her hand he was gripping upward until she wrapped it around his neck. His free hand curved around her waist, drawing her closer.

Damn. She smelled so good. And she was so soft, her skin so warm. Unable to help himself, he groaned into her mouth. It had been a long time since he'd been intimate with anyone. Even longer since he'd felt the heat of someone alive...or at least remembered it.

He tried to deepen the kiss, but Lacy giggled and pushed away from him. "We can't do it here, Grimm."

Alex frowned not only at her calling him by his last name, but also at the fact that she was using better judgment than he was at the moment. "Yes," he said stiffly, backing up a step and smoothing the towel at his waist as a distraction for his hands. "Yes. You are perfectly correct. It was inappropriate of me. I shouldn't have..." He trailed off in embarrassment. He shouldn't have what? Responded? She'd kissed him first, after all. If she didn't want... His thoughts trailed off as she giggled again.

"Oh, you definitely should have. And it was completely appropriate." She closed the small distance he'd put between them and walked her fingernails up his chest. "I thought it was your idea to consummate this marriage all over the city," she purred. "And we've already done it here. Time for a new location."

Alex choked on his next breath and eyed her nervously. "I what?" He gulped. "I said that?"

Lacy bobbed her head. "You sure did." Her other hand moved to the knot of his towel. "It was your idea to have sex in the elevator." She gave him a seductive look. "Though I did have the fun idea to head down to the pool room and...consummate in the hot tub."

She attempted to undo his towel, but Alex closed his hand over hers, halting her. "You're telling me we had sex in the elevator?" he hissed under his breath, as if afraid someone might hear him. His mind ran through all the horrible possibilities that situation presented. They could have been attacked. They could have been killed. They could have been *seen*.

Lacy ignored his near panic and pressed on. "The elevator, the hot tub, the pool, our shower, your car, the hotel bedroom...am I missing anywhere?"

Alex closed his eyes for a moment, trying to collect himself. *Exactly how much did I drink last night?* he silently asked himself. He'd been abstinent and alcohol-free for years, decades. Last night, he'd thrown all his morals out the window. He'd gotten married in Vegas, for crying out loud!

Straightening to his full height, Alex gripped his towel tightly against himself and said, "No. I think you've covered it all."

Clearing his throat, he edged past her toward his duffel bag. It was becoming quite apparent that he wasn't going to be able to brush this woman off. She was wearing his mother's wedding ring. It was going to take more than a few smooth words to get rid of her. "Be ready to leave in five minutes," he said gruffly, reluctantly giving in to her wish to accompany him.

Lacy beamed. "I'm going with you? You're letting me see you do some super-secret detective work?"

Alex nodded, distracted as he pulled a perfectly folded black t-shirt from his bag. "I suppose."

"Awesome!" she squealed, slipping on a pair of platform sandals.

He glanced down at her shoes and idly wondered how she would even be able to walk in them. "Yes, *awesome* was precisely the word I was looking for," he said sarcastically. It was going to be a long day.

Chapter Two

"I'm bored," Lacy groaned, dragging the second word out much longer than it ever should be. She crossed her legs in agitation and began bouncing her foot at an irritatingly quick tempo.

Alex glanced down in annoyance as the dirty bottom of her shoe repeatedly tapped against his pant leg. "Do you mind?" he asked darkly.

Lacy shot him a fiery look. "Actually, I do mind," she said shortly. "I'm a newlywed. I should not be sitting here on my ass, bored out of my mind. We should find a relatively private place and commence with the fucking."

Alex flinched. "Language," he chastised.

Her eyebrows shot practically to her hairline. "So now you're my fucking father?"

He flinched again and noticed with embarrassment that the old lady next to them got up and stormed off. "You're right. You're right," he rushed, trying to keep her from cursing again. "I'm being a terrible...husband." He struggled over the last word and tried to ignore the foul taste it left in his mouth. "It isn't your fault I have to work." He reached inside his wallet and pulled out two crisp hundred dollar bills. "Why don't you get some chips and do some gambling?"

Her aggravation apparently forgotten, Lacy snatched the bills from his hand and hopped to her feet with a perky bounce. "You're the best." She gave him a quick peck on the cheek before darting off.

Alex let out a sigh of relief as soon as she disappeared around a corner. With Lacy off doing her own thing, he could better concentrate. He was trying to pick out anomalies in the casino crowd. If there were supernatural creatures playing loan shark, they wouldn't behave entirely human. They usually had tells. He just needed to stay under the radar and pick them out.

"I got us some chips," Lacy declared happily as she dropped next to him on the seat in front of a quarter slot machine.

He hadn't considered that she'd return to do her gambling right next to him, mixing her pleasure with his business. He'd ignorantly assumed that she'd entertain herself for at least a few hours, not come running back to him like an over-energetic puppy. "Fantastic," he drawled.

Totally missing his sarcasm, she spun her chair to face the machine and fed it a few tokens.

Alex fought not to roll his eyes as he stayed facing the open room, his gaze flicking with scrutiny around the vast casino floor. Something caught his attention, and he zeroed in on a man across the room.

The man was leaning against the wall, staring into the casino as if surveying it himself.

Alex had superhuman night vision, so although the other man's eyes were hidden by shadows, he could still see him sweeping the crowd.

Alex leaned forward, wanting to get a better look. He jumped in surprise when arms suddenly wrapped around his neck. He grabbed one of the arms with every intention of breaking it. It was only when lips pressed against the side of his neck that he realized he wasn't under attack. It wasn't an assault, but an attempt at seduction. He halted his motions, barely able to stop himself in time. He'd been mere moments from doing something he'd probably regret later.

It was Lacy. She was on her knees on her chair, leaning over toward him. She caressed her hands down the front of his chest, tip-toeing her fingers along his shirt. Leaning in against his back, she kissed his neck again. "I'm not doing very good, babe." She nuzzled his right ear. "Maybe I need a few good luck smooches from you."

Alex tightened his grip on her wrist. "I almost broke your arm," he growled. He extracted himself from her and nudged her back into her own seat. "Are you crazy?"

"Crazy for you," she chirped.

He spun in his chair to glare at her. "I am trying to work. Could you please keep yourself entertained, at least for a little?"

Lacy pouted, but turned her attention back to the slot machine. "Jeez. What a grump."

He ignored her and spun back to look for the man he'd been observing. He almost growled when he could no longer find him. His gaze swept angrily over the area where he'd last seen the man.

He finally located him a few feet to the left of where he'd previously been. He'd met a woman at the doorway to the ladies room.

The woman smiled at the man, took his hand, and the two of them headed toward a row of slot machines.

The man had merely been waiting for his companion to get out of the rest room. Nothing more.

Alex was used to waiting long hours for results, so this didn't frustrate him in the least. Bad guys didn't just jump out at a person. He needed to have a trained eye and patience.

"Grimm," Lacy groaned, breaking his concentration once again. "I don't want to gamble by myself. We're newlyweds. We should be sneaking off to fuck in a closet or something instead of acting like total strangers. This has been forty minutes of you ignoring me. I want you to gamble *with* me, not sit me in front of a machine like it's a babysitter."

First, Alex flinched at her use of the F word. Then he felt irritation well up inside of him. Did she not realize that she was, in fact, a total stranger to him? He'd woken up to a nightmare. He wasn't the marrying type. Hell, he wasn't even the dating type. The only reason she was with him now was so he could force her to agree to an annulment the moment he had a chance to find someone with the authority to wipe their ridiculous marriage from the books like it never happened.

Instead of telling her this and causing a public argument, Alex shoved his hand roughly into the bucket of chips on her lap. "Fine," he seethed. Pulling out a chip, he spun in his chair to face the row of machines lined up along the wall behind him. He jammed the chip into the designated slot of the one in front of him, cursing under his breath. He slammed his palm into the button to start the machine. As soon as the colorful wheels started spinning, he turned his back, returning his attention to the rest of the room. "Happy?" he practically growled.

Lacy's eyes narrowed, and she opened her mouth as if to argue, but was interrupted by a loud, screeching siren.

Lights started flashing, reflecting off the ceiling to bounce in every direction.

It took Alex a moment to realize all the racket was coming from the machine behind him.

Lacy's head whipped in its direction. She gave a cry of delight and threw her arms around his neck. "You hit the jackpot!"

He turned in surprise to face her and, not for the first time since he'd awoken in her hotel room, she was suddenly kissing him.

Lacy's mouth was hot on his. Grabbing the front of his shirt, she scooted forward, practically putting herself in his lap.

Alex could feel her heart pounding excitedly in her chest against his own. She was so warm and tempting. As he responded to her kiss against his will, he could see how his drunken self could have fallen victim to her charms. She was enticing. She was appealing. She was downright addictive.

Just as he was giving in to the inevitable, Lacy jumped away from him with speed he would have thought belonged to a vampire. "My husband won!" Clamoring to her feet, she pointed frantically down at him. "My husband won! He won the jackpot! Bring him some money!" she cried dramatically, pumping a fist in the air. Her attention swiftly returned to Alex. "Thirty thousand dollars. Oh my God!"

Alex cringed. Grabbing her wrist, he yanked her back down into her chair. "Shh!" He looked behind him to see how much attention she was drawing. Being alive as long as he'd been gave a vampire time to build a small fortune. Thirty thousand dollars was nothing to him, and right now, it was drawing unwanted attention.

Due to all the whistles and bells, it didn't take long for a floor manager to be at the machine. "Congratulations," he said enthusiastically, patting Alex on the back. "You're a big winner." He began clapping his hands, motioning for those around him to join in. "Give him a hand, people!"

Alex couldn't stop his hackles from rising. "Don't touch me," he warned.

Lacy, on the other hand, seemed thrilled by the attention. She hopped up to stand on the seat of her chair and waved to the onlookers. "We won!" She gave a little curtsy, her bare leg brushing up against his shoulder.

Alex glanced up at her and groaned in embarrassment. His gaze flicked to the surrounding people to confirm his suspicions. Reaching up, he wrapped his thumb and forefinger easily around her wrist. "Please don't forget that you are wearing a miniskirt. You are drawing the attention of the entire male population of Vegas."

Lacy stumbled on her heels and nearly toppled off her chair. Giggling, she jumped down, her heels clomping loudly against the tile floor. "Are you jealous?" she sang, throwing her arms around his neck. "You could just snap all their necks for looking at me. Isn't that what you vampires do?"

Alex was momentarily distracted as she slid her body down his, but he quickly recovered. "Yes. That is exactly what we do. You shouldn't be so flippant about murder. You have no idea what I'm capable of, what I've done."

"You're too cute," was Lacy's response. Lowering her arm from around his neck, she playfully pinched his cheek.

He nearly growled in frustration. He'd been alive since the dark ages. Rational men feared him. He'd killed more people than he could even remember. It infuriated him that this girl, this child, didn't cower before him. Hell, she didn't even believe him.

Before Alex could do anything rash that he'd probably regret doing later, the floor manager distracted him with, "Who should we be making the check out to, sir?"

Alex tensed. He hated drawing any unwanted attention to himself. It was easier to cover his tracks if no one knew where he was. "Make it out to her," he rushed out, nodding to Lacy. "The money is hers."

Lacy inhaled sharply and turned to him with wide eyes. "You are the best husband ever!" She spun to the floor manager with a delighted squeal. "You can make it out to Lacy Grimm." She giggled at the name and held out her left hand to show off the ring on her finger. "We're newlyweds."

Alex raised his eyebrows at the fact that she'd taken his last name. Sure, it was still common practice in today's society, but it was odd hearing his last name attached to this woman.

"That's wonderful," the manager gushed. After verifying that they were staying in the attached hotel, he said, "To celebrate your good news, we are going to upgrade you to our honeymoon suite. How does that sound?"

"That sounds fantastic!" Lacy gushed, looking ready to explode from exhilaration.

"Why don't the two of you follow us to the office and we can get everything finalized," the manager suggested.

Alex waved him off. "My wife can handle everything. She's more than capable." He wasn't exactly sure what his new wife was capable of, but he would give her the benefit of the doubt. Letting her go collect their winnings might give him some uninterrupted time to do his job.

"Okay," Lacy eagerly agreed. "I'll go take care of this while you look for bad guys."

Before he could protest about her disclosure of his activities, she kissed him on the cheek and scampered off.

The moment she was out of sight, he dropped his head into his hands. He swore he felt a headache coming on, which was amazing. He hadn't had a headache in centuries, but Lacy, in all her insanity, was bringing one on. He was practically counting down the hours until it was feasible to get this farce of a marriage annulled.

Lacy would be walking away with thirty thousand dollars, so she couldn't get angry over their split. It wasn't as if she'd had time to form an attachment to him.

Alex was so wrapped up in how he was going to resolve the issue involving his nightmare marriage that he lost track of time. It wasn't until forty minutes later when Lacy plopped into his lap that he realized he hadn't done an ounce of work.

"Did I mention that you're the best husband ever?" she purred, nibbling gently at his earlobe.

Alex sucked in a rush of air and tensed. He sat up straight in his chair and clenched his hands into fists at his sides. "Lacy, is this really..." He gulped when her hands slid up his chest, her nails raking his skin through his shirt. "You...may have mentioned it," he said weakly.

Lacy's lips traveled along his jaw, leaving kisses as she went. "I'm taking that money and buying us a honeymoon." She finally found his mouth with hers and practically attacked. "We're going to Greece. It will be so unbelievably romantic. We've never been to Greece."

"I was born in Greece," Alex mumbled. His eyebrows furrowed, but that didn't stop him from letting her kiss him.

Lacy pulled back with a frown. "You were born there?"

Wanting to avoid unnecessary questions about his long ago past, Alex grabbed her waist and pulled her back toward him. "Greece is fine," he assured. "We can go to Greece." His hand moved to the back of her neck, and he pulled her down for another kiss.

It was about this time that he realized he'd just agreed to take a honeymoon with the woman he was trying to get out of his life. He just kept getting himself in deeper and deeper.

In warning, he mumbled against her lips, "I am not husband material. You'll be begging me for a divorce in a week if we let this go on any further. We should really—"

Lacy cut him off, finishing his sentence in a completely different way than he'd been about to. "Find somewhere new to have sex. I don't think I can wait a minute longer."

This broke what little resolve he had left. Lunging to his feet, he grabbed her arm and began tugging her in the direction of the bathrooms. Halfway there, his eyes landed on a coat closet, and he took a detour.

Tossing the door to the closet open, he glared daggers at the two workers who were hanging up a pile of jackets. "Get out," he growled.

Like any other human on the planet besides Lacy would, the two workers shrank back. "N...no problem," the oldest looking of the two mumbled, skirting his way around them to the exit. The second man followed, and the two of them raced out.

Alex pulled Lacy over to the counter overflowing with jackets too warm for the hot Nevada weather. Grabbing her hips, he lifted her to sit on the pile of coats.

"Ooh," she cooed. "Big, bad, scary vampire. It gives me tingles."

Alex growled in frustration. "I really wish you would take this more seriously. I could kill you at any moment. I'm terrifying."

"Mmm," Lacy mumbled, sliding her hands up his shirt to run her silky palms along his back. "Terrifying." With a giggle, she removed her hands from his shirt and reached up to run her hands through his short hair, straightening her back to arch up against him.

At her aggressive tug at his hair, Alex almost lost his balance. To steady himself, he pressed his hands against the counter on either side of her legs. "I'm serious," he said sternly. "I'm dangerous."

"Mmm-hmm, dangerous," she agreed. She shivered and made a noise of desire in the back of her throat. "A bad boy. I have to be careful I don't get burnt."

"We don't like fire," Alex responded automatically.

Lacy giggled. "Vampires. Sunlight. Fire." She giggled again, sounding almost drunk. "You guys have some crazy issues. I thought I was bad with my ex-boyfriend shit."

Alex broke away from her, oddly breathless for a vampire. "Ex-boyfriend issues?"

"Forget about it," she demanded, grabbing his arm and wrapping it around herself. "Just do me."

Alex saw no choice but to oblige. "Okay," he breathed into her mouth. And with that, he let go. It had been a lifetime since he'd been so tempted by a woman. He felt like a puppet, and Lacy was pulling all his strings.

His fingers tugged her t-shirt down over one shoulder, exposing creamy, tantalizing skin. He admired its perfection for a moment before lowering his mouth to her shoulder. He kissed it tenderly, then began kissing a steady path across her collarbone.

Lacy wrapped her long legs around his hips, giving a soft moan at his attention. "Bite me again." Her head tilted back invitingly. "I want your fangs in me. Bite me, Grimm."

Alex groaned. He felt his incisors extend, felt his entire body meld his predator instinct with his sexual arousal. With a growl, he lowered his mouth toward her throat, toward that succulent expanse of flesh that could curb his every desire.

He was inches from sinking his fangs deep into her throat when she suddenly sat up with a gasp. "Wait!"

Blinded by lust, Alex ran a hand over her hip and pulled her closer to him. "It's a little late for second thoughts, don't you think?"

Lacy put a hand to his chest and firmly pushed him back. "I'm not having second thoughts. There is nothing I want more than to have raunchy sex with you in this coat closet. It's just..." She gently removed the hand that was snaking its way toward her breasts. "I know how to find your vampires."

Alex yanked back, suddenly alert. "You do?" He realized how much sarcasm dripped from his voice, so he cleared his throat. "I mean, you do?" he asked, trying to sound encouraging.

"Yes," she gushed enthusiastically. "You need to go to the people who are the eyes and ears of this town." She shimmied out from under him and jumped down from the counter. "You go to the people who everyone speaks freely in front of because they aren't seen as a threat. They're just part of the background."

"I don't know who you're talking about," Alex said as he spun to face her when she headed for the door.

"Just...trust me."

He followed her, but grabbed her wrist to halt her when she was within reach. "Does this plan of yours involve leaving the hotel?"

Lacy stared up at him in confusion. "Yeah."

"Then it has to wait until sundown." He let go of her wrist to wrap his arm around her waist and pull her into his chest. "Relax. There's no need to go anywhere."

When he lowered his lips toward hers, she pressed her index finger to them. "I have research to do." Grabbing his hand, she pulled him through the closet door and back out to the gambling floor with her. "You said your job was very important, right? Then there's no time to waste."

"I did say that, didn't I?" he grumbled with reluctance. As Alex followed her through the crowd of people, he felt something unfamiliar to him. It started in his toes and crept up his body like ice. The unfamiliar sensation—sexual frustration.

Chapter Three

Alex stared up at the building in front of him in disbelief. "This was your big idea?" he asked with a groan of exasperation.

"It's going to work," Lacy informed him as she brushed by and entered the sophisticated structure.

"A spa?" he said skeptically as he stared up at the flashy sign. "Gabe's Spa and Salon. I have to be out of my mind." He rubbed his hands over his face to collect himself and then trailed after his new wife. Entering the spa, he looked around the lavishly feminine interior for Lacy.

She was at the reception desk talking to a petite brunette.

Feeling completely out of his element, Alex joined Lacy at the counter. Rubbing a hand against the back of his neck in an effort to mask his discomfort, he asked, "So what's on the agenda?"

Lacy spun to him with a beaming smile. "Well, first up, we're scheduled for a paraffin body wrap followed by an aromatherapy facial. Then we have spa manicures. Then to wrap things up, I scheduled me for a pedicure and you for a hair styling package. They'll do the whole deal—cut, dye, and style, basically whatever you want. You'll look downright edible when they're finished."

His eyebrows rose practically to his hairline. "No," he said simply, leaving no room for debate.

"No?" Lacy asked, blinking at him in puzzlement. "Would you prefer something else? I didn't peg you for a hot stone massage type of guy seeing as you don't like fire, but if you want..."

"No." Alex grabbed her elbow and pulled her a few feet away from the desk. "I meant no as in no to all of it. I am not getting—" He made a noise close to gagging. "A manicure. Absolutely not."

Lacy's eyes narrowed. "Do you want information or not?" Before he could answer, she stated, "If you do, then stop being such a little bitch."

"You don't even know if these people have a single piece of helpful information," he argued, his tone already sounding defeated.

"And you don't know that they don't." Her expression turned smug at his following silence. "That's what I thought. Now get your sexy ass in there and get naked for your body wrap."

"It appears I have no choice but to compromise with you or I'll be hearing about it the rest of the day, but I am not exposing myself to attack by being nude. I would be too far from my weapons."

"Pessimistic much?" she asked incredulously. "And you brought weapons to a hair stylist? Who do you think is doing your hair, Jackie Chan?" She sighed, giving up on the body wrap. "Facials?" she asked hopefully.

"How are you going to question them with goop all over your face? You just want a facial. It has nothing to do with questioning the people here. You know you aren't going to get any information during that silly thing."

Lacy frowned, but her lips quickly crept into a guilty grin. "You got me." Her hands went to her hips, and she stared daggers at him. "Okay. You can't say no to the manicure."

Alex hesitated. He felt like he was fighting a losing battle. She was going to get her way. No matter how much he fought, he had to give her something. Despite his best efforts, she was going to get him to behave like a sissy. He'd never even stepped into a spa before in his life. Now he was getting a manicure. "Damn it," he cursed.

Lacy blinked at him for a moment in surprise. "What?" she finally asked.

Alex sighed, his shoulders rounding in defeat. "Okay," he said glumly. "You win. I'll do it. Just know that this isn't going to be a recurring thing. I just want to prove you wrong, then get the hell out of here."

She bounced up and kissed his cheek. "You won't regret it." She spun and marched back over to the reception desk. "Okay. Scratch the order I started. Instead, we'll take two classic manicures." She glanced over her shoulder and gave Alex an impish grin before turning back to the receptionist. "Also, a cut and style for him and a spa pedicure for me, please."

Alex rolled his eyes. He hated just the sound of it.

Lacy took his hand and pulled him to follow the receptionist. She was practically quivering with excitement. "I am going to look so sexy with a French pedicure."

Alex thought she was pretty damn sexy without the stupid pedicure, but he just nodded in agreement.

They were lead to a long table and seated next to each other across from two pleasant-looking women.

Alex took his seat, trying to keep the disagreeable expression off his face as the woman across from him, whose nametag read Bethany, grabbed his hands and dipped them into an electric bowl filled with hot, bubbling water.

Next to him, Lacy let out a content sigh. "Heavenly," she murmured.

He grunted, finding nothing heavenly about the situation. "You know I'm just going to get them bloody on the first person I punch in the face," he warned his wife as his manicurist began cleaning his hands with a scrub brush. "This is truly pointless."

Lacy shot him a warning look due to the horror that flashed across both manicurists' faces. "Well, at least you'll look good for a few weeks, honey."

"A few weeks?" He scoffed at the idea. "You'll be lucky if I go a few days."

Bethany inhaled sharply, her fingers hesitating in their scrubbing, and she shot the second woman a quick, nervous glance.

Trying to diffuse the situation, Lacy leaned over and rested her head against Alex's shoulder for a moment. "My husband is a private detective," she explained to the women. "He has a very dangerous job. Bad guys don't like to play by the rules. They usually turn things violent. My husband has no option but to kick a little criminal ass sometimes." She beamed at him. "He's my hero."

The manicurists visibly relaxed. "How brave," the woman doing Lacy's nails, Sheila according to her nametag, gushed.

"More like stupid," Alex grumbled.

Lacy kicked him under the table. "Don't scare them off, bonehead," she hissed out of the corner of her mouth. "Try to be a little likable. Please?" She turned to the manicurists with a bright smile. "He's just being funny. He's got one of those British senses of humor."

Both women nodded as if they completely understood this.

"I'm not British," Alex complained half-heartedly.

The women seemed to relax due to Lacy's infectious smile. "I imagine you see some pretty crazy things in your line of work," Bethany said conversationally.

"Yes, I—" Alex didn't get to finish his sentence, because he was interrupted by Lacy.

"He sure does," she gushed. "He's always hunting the craziest bad guys! I mean, right now, he's working on this case involving evil vampires. *Evil vampires*. Can you believe it? I almost don't!"

Alex saw the look that shot between the two women. It wasn't just a look of people who thought you were crazy. It was a look of people who knew something. Damn it all if Lacy hadn't been right.

Lacy must have seen the look too, because she said, "You guys look like you know what I'm talking about."

Shelia hesitated, the cuticle pusher in her hand frozen in uncertainty. "Well...we hear things..."

Lacy's eyes widened in intrigue. "No!" She said this with mock surprise, as if she couldn't believe the coincidence. She bounced in her seat, seemingly at ease, while Alex tensed in anticipation. "Tell," she demanded playfully. "If you know where we can find one of those bullies, Grimm will have them off the streets before you know it. You could help save lives!"

Though "bully" was a very watered down description of these vampires, Alex felt as if she was getting somewhere. She was doing well.

The manicurists glanced at each other uncertainly before Bethany turned to look at Alex and said, "There's been a vampire who comes in here every so often and threatens

Gabriel."

"Gabriel?" Alex asked. "As in Gabe the owner?"

Both women bobbed their heads emphatically. Sheila glanced behind her as if making sure no one was listening in on their conversation. "Okay. So this vampire has been coming in here over the last year with a group of thugs, and he's been threatening Gabriel. He's demanding a quarter of our profits. Gabe wanted to fight them on the issue, but..." She shrugged. "He was worried about everyone's safety. About ten months ago, he started paying them. He's been fudging the records he provides to them, and he never includes our tips. Even so, these guys are getting a decent fifteen percent."

"Any clue why they would target this place, target your boss?"

Both women instantly grew tense and clammed up. In the silence, they shot each other looks of concern.

"What is it?" Lacy persisted. "We can help. You just need to guide us in the right direction."

Bethany stopped grooming Alex's hands and took them in hers, her eyes intent on his and serious. "Gabriel is a vampire," she whispered.

Sheila was quick to add, "He's not a bad vampire, though. He just wants to run his business and be left alone."

"These vampires told him they run this city, that if any other vampire wanted to do business here, they were going to get their cut," Bethany added.

Alex tried to keep his expression from looking too eager. "We're going to need to talk to your boss. If everything you say is true, I can help."

Bethany shrugged and returned her attention to his manicure. "You're scheduled for a hair session with him as soon as we finish up here. I'm sure he'd be more than willing to give you some information."

Alex fought not to roll his eyes. A hair session? His hair was short. Apart from the spikes he normally wore it in, there wasn't much to be done with it. Without giving him a buzz cut, there wasn't much they could change, though he would play along for the sake of possibly getting valuable information.

He spent the rest of his manicure not relaxing as the treatment advertised, but preparing himself for his coming conversation with Gabriel. Vampires were not known for being forthcoming with one another. In fact, they could be downright guarded in regard to each other. And there wasn't much sense in even trying to pretend he wasn't a member of the walking dead community. Vampires could practically spot each other from a mile away.

Alex wasn't sure how he was going to be able to get anything useful out of this. And if he *did*, he wondered what it would cost him.

Sheila pulled him out of his thoughts as she sat Lacy's hands down on the table and climbed to her feet. "You're all finished, miss," she said politely. "If you'll excuse me, I'm going to go run the water for your pedicure." She then made a hasty retreat into a connecting room, closing the door behind her.

Alex knew she was going to give her boss a heads up, but he didn't blame her. Actually, it was probably better this way. A vampire caught unaware usually turned violent.

Presumably thinking her co-worker was doing as much and wanting to give her own input, Bethany quickly finished up with his hands. Climbing hurriedly to her feet, she said, "I'll go tell Gabriel to prepare for your hair session." She cut across the floor and disappeared through the same door as Sheila.

As soon as the door closed behind her, Lacy squealed and nudged his leg with her own. "I told you this would work! This is exciting, isn't it?"

His response was a frown. "Exciting? No. It is not exciting. Potentially dangerous, yes. Exciting, no. Excitement insinuates fun. This is my job. I am working right now, not having fun." On her look of deflation, he relented some, trying to be a little more sensitive. "Thank you for this lead. I greatly appreciate it...even if I was *forced* into a manicure."

Her bright smile returned. "I did good, didn't I?" she asked proudly.

Alex couldn't help but give her a soft smile in return. "You did good." Unable to help himself, he reached out and tucked an errant lock of hair behind her ear. "I still can't believe out of all the spas in this city, you managed to find the one run by a vampire. What made you pick this place?" he asked curiously.

She gave a coy smile. "My research this afternoon. I looked for the place whose hours were mostly after dark. I know this city never sleeps, but this place was setting off all kinds of bells. An owner who you can't book an appointment with until after nine? It could have been nothing, but if a vampire is going to be running a business, these are the hours I'd expect from them. It just seemed fishy."

Alex grabbed her face in his hands. "That's genius!" Overcome with excitement, he leaned forward and gave her a firm kiss. "I never would have thought to check somewhere so...mundane."

One of Lacy's arms slid around his neck. She leaned in and pecked his nose with a kiss. "You're welcome." Her mouth moved to his cheek. "Anything for my vampire," she whispered in his ear.

Alex growled, his fangs tingling at her comment. He was just leaning his mouth over her neck when someone behind them cleared their throat. He turned his head slowly to see Bethany.

"Gabriel will see you now." She was trying for neutral, but he could hear the amusement in her voice at their intimate behavior.

He closed his eyes for a moment to collect himself. "One of these days, I'm going to bite you," he said under his breath.

"I hope so," she whispered back.

The eagerness in her voice sent a shiver down his spine, but Alex set her with a serious look. "If it sounds like it's turning violent, I want you to take off. Head back to the hotel and wait for me."

Lacy slapped him playfully in the chest. "Vampires. You're all so dramatic. Try not to make it a pissing contest. That might help."

Alex glared at her. First off, *all* vampires? She didn't even know any besides him, and she didn't even know *him* that well. Second, pissing contest? Was it his fault the people he questioned weren't forthcoming with information? No. Sometimes it was necessary to put a little fear into people to get them to cooperate. "Just do as I say," he growled.

Without waiting for a response, he got up and followed Bethany into the connecting room. He tried to hold back his groan at the sight that greeted him.

There were curlers and scissors and perm kits and those giant hair dryers everywhere. It was a man's worst nightmare.

Except the man leaning against the wall looked every bit at home. He looked proud of his surroundings.

The man Alex assumed was Gabriel appeared to be in his mid-forties. His hair was jet black with streaks of gray at the temples. His eyes were hazel, searching Alex through wisps of hair that hung over his forehead. His clothes were a dark gray and obviously expensive.

"I'm assuming you're Gabe," Alex said evenly.

The man smirked in amusement. "The one and only."

"Do you prefer Gabe or Gabriel?" Alex asked, trying to appear as unthreatening as possible.

Gabriel's grin widened. "Well, the women call me Gabriel. My lover Stanford calls me Gabe. Which are you, a woman or a lover?"

Alex froze. He fought to keep his jaw from hitting the floor. Was this man trying to get into his head or...

Gabriel let out a delighted laugh. "Vampires, always so serious." He pushed away from the wall and started toward Alex. "You can call me Gabriel." He held out a hand. "Besides, Stanford would hunt you down and set you on fire if you made a pass at me."

Alex was so stunned it took him a moment to find his voice. "Y...you're gay?" He frowned, looking around him in disbelief. "Is this some kind of joke?"

"No joke. I'm gay. Very much so," Gabriel disclosed as Alex finally shook his hand. "Did you think there were no vampires like me wandering about?"

"What?" Alex said with a harsh laugh. "Gay vampires? Can't say I did."

"Straight men," Gabriel complained, "so close-minded, so self-centered."

Alex crossed his arms over his chest and glowered. He wasn't prepared to handle this situation at all. Snarling and brawling he was familiar with. He didn't have the first clue about how to handle a homosexual vampire.

Gabriel sighed in disappointment. "Okay. I can see your sense of humor is all of non-existent. Let's move on to the death and horror." He motioned toward a seat, which would lean the person using it over a sink. "And let's not forget your hair."

Alex ran a hand anxiously though his spikes. "Perhaps we could skip the hair."

Gabriel made a *tsk* noise. "Heavens no. If I'm going to be forced into talking about such barbaric things, the least you can do is let me help you look fabulous while we do so."

Fearing for his masculinity, Alex cautiously approached the chair.

When Alex was close enough, Gabriel pulled him down into the seat. "You're going to look smashing, while I will be less tense because I'll have these threats off my chest. It's a win for both of us."

He grabbed the extendable sprayer connected to the sink, gave Alex's hair a thorough spray, and then began lathering it in shampoo. "So, this vampire started coming in here last year. He's obviously low card and a horrible dresser." Gabriel snickered. "He was wearing these awful burnt orange corduroy pants. He looked like he'd died in the seventies and hadn't found the time to change. I could barely stand to look...at...him..." He trailed off slowly at Alex's dirty look. "Right...you don't care about that."

Moving Alex to a sitting position, Gabriel grabbed a small bowl from the shelf hanging along the wall to his left. He partially filled the bowl with a bottled liquid. He then began mixing a powder into it, creating a paste-like substance. "The guy's name is Walter. He calls himself the Bear. Don't ask me why. Personally, I don't want to find out. It sounds violent."

Using what Alex could only describe as a spatula, Gabriel began slopping the goop into his hair.

"Anyway," Gabriel continued, "the Bear comes in here and tells me that the head honcho vampire in Vegas doesn't appreciate me setting up shop and making a profit in his territory. I'm to give him a cut, or I'm to get lost."

With focused attention, Gabriel began smoothing the substance on Alex's head into hair he was targeting. "I finally came to realize that it was best to just pay these men. I don't want any trouble. And the girls are human. I don't even want to think about what a man like Walter would do to them if he were unhappy with us."

"Do you know where I can find Walter?" Alex asked. His

nose curled in disgust at the odor permeating from his head. He made a point to cease all breathing. It was unnecessary for a vampire to continue breathing once they'd been turned. Most did it solely out of the habit of trying to blend in. Seeing as that was uncalled for here, Alex made the effort to halt his lungs' intake of the tainted oxygen wafting down from his hair.

"Walter runs a pretty shady business from a dance club he owns. I've heard rumors..." Gabriel paused, fidgeting anxiously with his spatula. "People disappear from there. The rumor is that he tricks humans into blood contracts. The silly things don't even realize what they're agreeing to. He lures them in for the head guy. They'll give the humans whatever they want—drugs, money, sex. These guys have their hands in everything."

Alex felt his blood boil. He knew without a doubt that this was the group responsible for Darlie's death. They were responsible for all of the trouble in this city that stemmed from vampires. If it was the last thing he did, he would hunt down and stake each and every one of these bastards. "What's the name of the club?" he growled.

"It's called the Nocturnal Lady." Gabriel stepped back and crossed his arms over his wide chest. "You don't actually plan on going there, do you? These guys aren't a joke. They're dangerous."

"I'm dangerous," Alex countered with a snarl.

"You came in for a manicure and a hair consult," Gabriel pointed out skeptically.

Alex felt his hackles rise. "I'm only going through with this garbage because my wife begged me to play nice. Had I been on my own, I would have beaten the information out of you, not gotten a manicure."

Gabriel gulped and took a step back. "Oh...lovely woman. I'm glad she decided to join us this afternoon. I think I'm going to set her up with a discount, possibly a few gift cards."

Alex tried to look as threatening as he possibly could with goop in his hair. "Good, because she will be the reason your business is no longer harassed."

Gabriel cleared his throat nervously. "Like I said, a lovely woman." He moved in cautiously to tip Alex back over the sink. His hands moving cagily, as if waiting for an attack, he began rinsing the sludge from Alex's hair.

Alex drummed his fingers impatiently on the arm handles of the chair as Gabriel plugged in a hair dryer. "The quicker we get to these guys, the sooner your business is back on track. I'm sure we can both agree that the blow thingy is unnecessary."

When Alex shifted the seat to an upright position and tried to stand, Gabriel shoved him back into the chair. "It is absolutely necessary." He blasted Alex for a good thirty seconds, drowning out any protests. When he turned off the hair dryer, he added, "Besides, I want to see the finished product, dried and spiked with gel."

Alex fidgeted. "Gel? I don't use gel." The most effort he'd ever put into his hair was running his wet hands through it to get it to make messy spikes.

Gabriel squirted a dab of green gel into his hand. "Welcome to the world of hair products."

Alex sat frozen. He was more nervous now than he would be when tracking down the Bear. Logically, he knew nothing bad would come from a little hair gel, but he still didn't like it. He was a simple guy. Gel seemed too high maintenance for him.

After a few moments of teasing Alex's hair into perfect shape, Gabriel stepped back. "Walla! You are a masterpiece." He motioned for Alex to stand. "Take a look."

Alex climbed to his feet and approached the mirror just to avoid an argument. He didn't really care how it looked. That was until he saw it. The sight of his hair caused him to freeze. His jaw dropped, and he stared in disbelief. His hair was blue.

He whirled on Gabriel, his eyes wide with outrage. "It's blue!" he hollered. He spun back to the mirror, hoping his image would change. It didn't. The bottom was still coal black, but the tips were blue. "It's fucking blue!" he cried.

Gabriel clapped his hands together, looking as jolly as could be. "Divine, isn't it?"

Alex whipped back to Gabriel. "Divine?" he cried, unable to keep himself from freaking out. "Divine?"

A high-pitched shriek from Lacy interrupted any response Gabriel might have been about to give.

Alex turned to her, his eyebrows raised as if to say *It's terrible, right?*

"Oh my God!" Lacy yelled, one of her hands flying up to cover her chest.

Alex felt justified in his negative reaction until Lacy raced toward him and jumped into his arms.

Her legs wrapped around his hips, her arms around his neck. "You look absolutely fucking sexy!" She ran her hands through his blue-tipped hair. "I love it!" She leaned in and kissed him forcefully. "Absolutely *love* it," she growled, biting his lower lip with desire. When she pulled back, she looked to Gabriel. "You are amazing!"

"I know," he came back smugly.

"Yeah, yeah," Alex grumbled. "Just tell me what I owe you so we can get to work on your little problem." As he said this, his mind argued with his words. He couldn't believe he was going to pay for the atrocity that had been done to his hair.

Gabriel waved him off. "If you're really going to help us as you claim, then you owe me nothing." He turned to Lacy with a warmer smile than he'd given Alex all day. "Free services for life for you, my dear treasure."

She beamed, not noticing as Alex lowered her feet to the floor. "What about my unlife when Grimm turns me into a vampire?" she asked playfully.

"Even then," Gabriel replied, pinching her cheek.

Alex didn't find her comment to be so cute. He found it to be a little too bold and presuming. "Lacy," he growled in disapproval.

She responded with a frown. "What? Like we all don't know it's gonna happen. You can't live without me."

"I'm not even alive," he countered dryly.

"Whatever," she said, unaffected by his logic. Her attention returned to Gabriel. "You're an absolute sweetheart." Reaching a hand out, she covered one of his with her own. "Grimm and I will put a stop to this harassment. You can count on us." With that said, she spun to Alex. "Let's go, baby. We have work to do."

Alex watched her saunter out the door. Irritation welled inside of him. No one told him what to do. He left a place when he felt he was finished. He didn't follow the orders of others, especially not someone wearing platform sandals and hot pink. Just to be stubborn, he planted his feet and scowled in the direction Lacy had disappeared.

Unaware of the standoff, Gabriel whistled. "Man oh man. That girl is one hot tamale." He tilted his head to the side to admire Lacy's backside as she disappeared out the door. "If I wasn't in a committed relationship with a man..."

Alex shot him an aggravated look. He may not have asked to be attached to Lacy, but she was still *his* wife. He didn't appreciate other men ogling her. And if gay men were checking out her ass, he was in trouble. "If you keep looking at my wife like that, I may change my mind and kick your ass for the fun of it."

Gabriel's eyes quickly shifted back to look at Alex, his expression guilty. "You're the boss."

Alex snorted his annoyance and gave up. He followed Lacy out the door.

She met him on the sidewalk outside, bouncing excitedly on her heels. "We did it! We have a lead."

Alex ignored her exuberance and started down the road where his car was parked in a garage. When she fell into step next to him, he grumbled, "Could you not call me pet names in public? It undermines my intimidation factor." He paused, annoyance brewing in him as he relived in his mind the moment when she called him *baby* in front of another vampire. "On second thought, could you not call me pet names ever?"

Lacy's expression became thoughtful. Then she shook her head. "Nope. I gotta do it. You're too adorable not to be called by a pet name. I will try to minimize the use in public, but that's the best I can guarantee."

He felt a twitch start in his eye. His nerves were jumping due to the stress she was putting him under. People didn't tell him *no*. They either cowered and agreed with him, or there was a fight to the death, their death that is. He glanced at Lacy.

She strolled along happily beside him as they entered the parking garage, completely unaware of what she was putting him through. She was far too...innocent, pretty, bubbly. She smelled too good to fight to the death.

Alex growled under his breath. He was stuck. He'd never wanted this, but he was in too deep to just up and leave her.

"So, what's the plan now?" she chirped. "Are we going to the club?"

"I need to think," Alex said quietly. "The club can wait until tomorrow." He shot her a pointed look as they approached his car. "As I said, I will need time to think. It would be greatly appreciated if you would..." It was at this time that he realized she was no longer listening to him. She was staring off into the parking lot with an intensity he'd never seen. "Lacy?" he asked.

"Do you have a tire iron in your car?"

The question threw him completely off guard. "Yes," he said slowly. He gaped at her for a moment, awaiting an explanation. "Why?" he finally asked.

"Can I see it?"

He blinked in surprise. "Well...I suppose." He popped the trunk to his car and pulled out the object in question. "But I don't know why you would want to—" He broke off when she snatched the tire iron from his hand.

She marched purposefully toward a row of cars two aisles over. Stopping in front of a silver Porsche, she widened her stance and swung the tire iron as if it were a baseball bat.

The metal crashed into the left taillight. The sound of shattering plastic and glass followed. Shards of busted taillight hit the pavement at her feet like rain.

"Lacy!" Alex cried in disbelief when the car's alarm system began screaming, the sound echoing off the cement walls of the garage. He raced to her side, his expression frantic. "What the hell are you doing?"

Ignoring him, she pulled the unforgiving piece of metal back and slammed it through the back driver side window. "Fuck you, Bernard!" Moving to the second window on that side, she made short work of it as well. Glass spilled into the car, covering the seats. The once flashy vehicle was now in dire need of repair. Not finished, she moved with intention to the windshield.

She lifted the tire iron over her head and was on her sadistic downward swing when Alex's hands shot out and grabbed it. He halted its destructive progress, his forearm straining with the sudden connection of metal with his palm. "What the hell is this about?"

Lacy took a stumbling step backwards, her breathing labored and her expression one of rage. Through heaving breaths, she huffed, "Remember those ex-boyfriend issues?"

She nodded her head toward the car.

"This is your ex-boyfriend's car?" he cried, his voice re-verberating along with the car's high-pitched squeals. He cursed under his breath. "What the hell is your ex-boyfriend doing in Vegas?"

Lacy's cheeks flushed. "Getting married," she practically whispered.

Alex threw his free hand up in frustration. "*Getting married*?" He shook his head in disgust. "So what, you decided to beat him to the punch?"

Her chin dipped for a moment. Then she raised it defiant-ly. "No!" She moved to his side and put a delicate hand on his arm. "It wasn't like that at all. You and I, it had nothing to do with dumb-ass Bernard."

Alex crossed his arms over his chest and directed a look of annoyance at her. He didn't know why it bothered him so much that she'd reacted to her ex getting married by throw-ing herself into her relationship with him. It wasn't like he even wanted to be married. He was planning on getting the stupid thing annulled as soon as he possibly could. It shouldn't bother him, but it did. "So you planned to get drunk off your ass and marry a perfect stranger?"

"No!" She snorted in aggravation and stomped a foot. "It just happened, alright? You and I both made a very reckless, hasty decision, but I don't regret it for a second, okay?"

Alex felt his hackles lower slightly. She didn't regret her decision. Deep down, he knew, if anything, she should be angry with him. He was annoyed with his situation, so he was projecting that annoyance onto her. He wasn't being fair. He intended to break her heart very soon. The least he could do was not be a total asshole to her during their brief marriage. When the time was right, he would set her down and calmly discuss going their separate ways.

Lacy was staring up at him with pleading eyes. "I mean, fuck Bernard. Right?"

Alex gave her a soft smile, his anger dissipating. "Fuck Bernard," he agreed.

Her smile was worth his surrender. He might not plan on living a happily ever after with her, but damn, he loved to see this woman smile. "Would you like to kick the car one last time for good measure?" he asked playfully.

Lacy moved forward on her heels and gave a spiteful kick to the fender, leaving a small dent. "That makes me feel good." She stepped in against Alex's side, wrapping her arm around his waist and nuzzling her head against his chest.

His arm slid automatically around her shoulders. "Let's get back to the hotel and check out that fancy new room."

Lacy bumped her hip playfully against his. "Sounds like fun." She gave him a wicked grin. "And for letting me take my frustrations out on Bernard's car, perhaps I'll have to make *you* feel good in return."

The sexual innuendo was thick in the air, and Alex had to swallow back a lump in his throat. *Damn* was the only thing he could think. As part of a married couple, she would expect sex, and he had no idea where to even begin. Last night's drunken blur excluded, it had been so long since he'd been intimate with another person. His lack of recent experience and insecurities about the subject would surely make any attempt a disaster. Feeling almost panicked, he made the decision to steer the situation away from sex at all costs. He just had to find a way to keep her distracted.

Chapter Four

Alex unlocked the door to the honeymoon suite he and Lacy had been upgraded to. As soon as he stepped inside, his eyes widened. The hotel room was nearly as big as his apartment. He enjoyed nice things, but *damn*.

"Oh my God," Lacy squealed. She ran through the large foyer into the connecting bedroom. "This place is amazing!"

Alex followed her at a more subdued pace. He leaned against the doorframe and smiled affectionately. "It is definitely nice."

Lacy kicked off her heels and threw herself face-first onto the massive bed. "This is *so* much better than my shitty apartment in Boston."

"Boston?" he asked in surprise, raising an eyebrow.

She rolled over onto her back so she could look at him. "I know what you're thinking. No accent. I make it a habit to keep it under control, though I can use it if you find it to be a turn-on." She winked. "If you're just looking to make me feel at home, I'd much rather get you naked and lick the filling of a Boston cream pie off your chest."

His hand flew to his chest in alarm. "That sounds rather messy." Trying to steer the conversation away from the combination of his chest and sticky pie filling, he said, "I was just surprised that you're from Boston. I never stopped to think that we might be from separate states."

On her frown, an idea occurred to him, and his lips curved into a malevolent smirk. "I mean, Boston and Green Bay are pretty far away from one another. Are you sure you want to move? I would understand *completely* if you would need to call this off. Your entire family must be in Boston."

He knew it was cruel to force her to choose between him and her family, but perhaps it would put things into perspective. Hopefully, she would realize that this was too big of a commitment to someone she barely knew. They could mutually break this whole marriage thing off, and no one would have to get hurt.

After practically mapping out how the conversation would go, he was thrown back to square one by her response.

"Well...I do love the Packers."

Alex huffed in annoyance. "But what about your family?"

Climbing to her knees on the bed, she shrugged. "Both of my parents died in a boating accident when I was four. My aunt, who is a nasty bitch, raised me. I spent the majority of my life at boarding schools. She despised me, hated the few weeks a year we were forced to spend together. She blew through my entire inheritance paying for schooling we really couldn't afford." She shrugged. "The few times a year I was home, I felt like Cinderella...only with better hair. There's nothing in Boston I'll miss."

Alex took her childhood story like a blow to the gut. What an awful life. There'd been no one around to look out for this sweet girl, to keep her safe from the harshness of the world. He made his way to her side in two strides of his long legs. Before he could think on what he was doing, he'd cupped her face in his hands. "You never have to go back to Boston. Ever." With that, he pressed his lips gently to hers.

It was Lacy who finally pulled back. "Thanks," she chirped, seemingly not bothered by the tale of her tragic childhood. Her eyes lit with excitement as she climbed to her feet and began jumping on the bed. "Can I get one of those big cheese hats? Those things are so crazy."

He shook his head, amused that all it took to make this woman happy was a foam hat made to look like cheese. "Yeah," he said with a soft smile. "I'll get you a cheese hat."

"Yippie!" She began jumping even higher, and he worried she might hit her head on the ceiling. He quickly forgot about the ceiling, though, when she pulled her t-shirt up over her head. "What are you doing?" he asked, sounding more frantic than he would have liked.

A wicked grin crept up her lips. "Afraid I'm trying to seduce you?" Before he could answer, she said, "I see a hot tub on the deck. We're going in."

Alex frowned. He'd never been in a hot tub before, and he didn't intend to try it now. "I don't own swimming trunks." Another thing he didn't intend to do any time soon.

"You could always go naked like you did at the pool last night," Lacy teased.

He tensed at her comment. Was there a single way in which he hadn't tried to embarrass himself the previous evening? "I will not be going naked," he informed her stiffly.

"Looks like you have two options then," she informed him. "You either go in your boxers or run down to the gift shop and buy some trunks." She slid her skirt down over her hips and kicked it to the floor. "Either way, you'd better be in that hot tub in less than five minutes."

Alex huffed in annoyance. She was a bossy little thing, but at least this would keep her thoughts from wandering to sex. For this, he would indulge her. "Fine," he practically barked. "Get your bathing suit on."

Lacy squealed and hopped down from the bed in excitement. "What to wear. What to wear."

His gaze shot to her as he lifted his t-shirt over his head. "You brought more than one bathing suit?"

Her responding expression was as if he had said something scandalous. "Of course I did! I have one for every occasion. You can never come too prepared. I have them in pink, red, white, black, and floral print."

"What is it with you and all the pink?" he grumbled.

She ignored this and pressed on. "I have one for outdoor sports, such as volleyball. I have a period bathing suit, a family appropriate bathing suit, a sunny suit, a nighttime suit, and my slutty bikini. Which do you want to see?"

"I don't care. Just pick one," he grumbled as he kicked his shoes off, nudging them into a corner.

"Okay," she chirped. "I'll surprise you."

Alex waved her off as he unbuttoned his slacks and stepped out of them. He left them on the floor in the middle of the room, because he knew that was exactly what Lacy was about to do. He hated to admit it, but it was somewhat liberating to leave something lay about. His life revolved around rules and regulations. He was almost a slave to it.

With a grunt of annoyance at his self-observation, he entered the deck in nothing but his boxers from a sliding door along the side wall of their room.

He had to admit, the deck was nice. It was a cherry, finished wood, open to the night sky, and was dimly lit by the flashing lights of the street far below. A wooden lid covered the hot tub.

It only took him a moment to get it uncovered and the water heating.

While Lacy did whatever it was that was taking her so long, Alex sunk into the warm water, relishing his few minutes of silence. His head tilted back, and he closed his eyes. While he relaxed, he ran his case through his mind.

Darlie was dead, but that didn't mean he was going to just turn his back and walk away. He didn't know his client personally, but that didn't matter. Someone had to keep the supernatural community in balance.

His thoughts moved to the dance club, the Nocturnal Lady. He would go. He would find Walter the Bear and work his way up the ladder. That seemed to be his only option at the moment.

"You look lost in thought. Or are you asleep?"

Alex jumped at the sound of Lacy's voice, and his eyes flew open. "Sorry. I was thinking." His gaze landed on her, finally taking her in, and his eyes widened.

She was in a skimpy, white bikini that set off the bronzed color of her skin nicely. With her hair shining in the moonlight and the glow of her skin, she looked like a Greek Goddess.

The bikini was the tiniest thing he'd ever seen. Her breasts peeked from around the outer sides of the flimsy top. Her abdomen was bare to the world, the muscles agreeably defined. A small, diamond belly button ring glittered in the light, reflecting off the water in the hot tub.

"Like it?" she asked sweetly, her voice sounding like something that should be coming from an angel.

She spun to show Alex the back, and his jaw nearly dropped. The back was a thong, showing off the sleek curves of her ass. "N-no tan lines," Alex stuttered.

She grinned at him over her shoulder. "I prefer to tan in the nude."

His heart, which normally didn't even bother to beat,

dropped to his toes. "Damn," he breathed.

With a grin, she slid into the hot tub, taking the seat across from him. "I'm going to have to start hitting the tanning beds because I hang out with you. You don't exactly keep daylight hours."

Alex had a coughing fit. "You tan in the nude *outside*?" he struggled to get out.

She winked. "Sure do."

"You're not worried someone might see you?" he asked, his voice an octave higher than usual.

"Maybe I'm *hoping* someone will see me," she purred suggestively. "Right now, for instance..." She slid closer to him on the circular seat, eyes glimmering wickedly. Her hand went to the tie at the neck of her bikini, and with a quick tug, it came undone. She let the fabric fall, exposing her equally tanned breasts. "I'm hoping a certain vampire gets more than an eyeful." She tugged the knot at her back, and her bikini top came completely off, floating away uselessly in the water.

Alex gulped, shoving back as far as he could in his seat. This wasn't exactly what he'd planned. He'd thought he could distract her from sex by indulging her wishes to get into the hot tub. He hadn't thought about the fact that they were under the stars and things looked terribly romantic out on this deck with the city sparkling below.

He had a moment to realize his plan had backfired, and then Lacy was climbing onto his lap.

She straddled his hips, leaning over him with a purr. "I've been wanting to do this all day," she whispered in his ear.

Alex grabbed her waist in an attempt to politely push her off of him, but he froze the moment his hands touched her skin. She felt like silk under his fingertips and smelled like strawberries. He had the fleeting thought that perhaps it wouldn't be so bad if they were to have a few stolen moments of passion.

His good sense tried to fight against his sudden new desire. If they slept together, it would only strengthen her attachment to him. It was a terrible idea.

Lacy leaned closer and grazed her lips across the stubble at his jaw line. As she did this, her breasts brushed against his chest.

"Lacy," he practically groaned. "This is a bad idea. We—"

She shifted on top of him, settling more tightly against the front of his boxers.

In that instant, all rational thought flew from his mind. His grip on her tightened, and he pulled her closer to him. His mouth somehow found hers, and he kissed her with enough force to bruise.

Lacy gave a squeak of surprise, but it quickly turned into a giggle. "Vicious," she purred teasingly.

"Shut up and kiss me," he demanded.

Lacy obliged. She wrapped her arms around his neck and attacked. Her lips pressed to his, and she rocked her hips forward.

Alex slid his hands up her waist, running his fingertips along her ribcage.

Her hands lifted to the top of her head, and she arched her back so that her breasts jutted up and into his chest. She'd moved her mouth from his only so that she could lean back to look at him. "Mmm...touch me," she breathed, her eyes fluttering closed. "Taste me."

This was a request he was more than happy to obey. He lowered his mouth over her throat, sucking gently at the skin. He tasted the salty flavor of her, teasing her with soft flicks of his tongue. While his mouth explored the graceful curve of her neck, his palms slid upward until he cupped her breasts.

It had been longer than he could remember since he'd been this close to a woman, this turned on. "My God, you're perfect," he breathed in awe.

Lacy leveled him with an intense gaze of her bright blue eyes. "And I'm yours, all yours."

Alex couldn't help the possessive growl that escaped him. The demon in him wanted to stake his claim, wanted to make sure her statement was true. She was his, and he wanted her.

"Grimm," she whispered in a breathy voice, pressing her breasts forward into his hands, "bite me."

Alex blanched, though his fangs sprang forward, demanding that he bleed her. His fangs were begging him to tear into her throat, to feel her blood roll down his tongue like a fine wine. "You don't know what you're asking of me," he managed to get out, his voice sounding thick with his effort to restrain himself.

Alex knew he couldn't do this. As much as his body was screaming at him to, he couldn't drink from Lacy. The romanticized version of vampires she probably had in her head was more than likely worlds away from the reality. He wasn't even sure if she truly believed him about his nature. He couldn't take advantage of her like that.

"I do know what I'm asking," she protested. "I want you to do what you did last night. That was better than any foreplay I've ever had." She rocked her hips forward as if begging him. "Please. I want you to."

Alex suddenly remembered the marks on her throat from this morning. She was right. He had fed from her before. And like this morning, a flash of memory returned to him. It wasn't just of him drinking. It was of him plunging between her legs as he fed. He could hear her desperate moans echoing in his mind.

His hands tightened on her breasts, teasing the soft mounds of flesh. "Like last night?" he asked, feeling his fangs thick against his tongue.

"Like last night," Lacy agreed. She lowered her hands between them and slid them into his boxer shorts. She gripped him in her tiny fists and squeezed.

Alex groaned, his head falling back for a moment at the sensation of her warm skin on him. He recovered enough to tug persistently at her bikini bottoms.

With much fumbling, and her giggling in his ear, they managed to get out of their clothing. Far beyond rational thought, Alex grabbed her hips and helped lower her onto his aching erection. He groaned again as he slid into her warm, inviting depths.

"Fuck, Grimm," she growled. "That is amazing." She moved on top of him, her rhythm slow, teasing. "Bite me now," she begged. "Bite me. Bite me." With every sentence, she arched up into his chest, sliding him in and out of her.

Alex couldn't hold back any longer. Lowering his mouth over her throat, he slid his fangs into a vein close to the surface. As soon as the sweet taste of her blood invaded his mouth, he grabbed her hips and yanked her forcefully down onto him.

Lacy cried out in pleasure and increased her rhythm to

the faster, rougher pace he coaxed her into. Her head tilted to the side, giving him better access.

Before long, Alex felt her body quiver and could tell by the pounding of her heart that she was approaching orgasm. He was surprised by her intense reaction. His past experience wasn't anything to brag about, and aside from last night, it had been a *really* long time, though that didn't seem to matter. Sexually, they just clicked.

He gripped her hips even tighter until his fingers left imprints in her skin. He drew in another mouthful of blood, savoring the flavor as it coursed its way down his throat. As he swallowed, they both reached climax.

Lacy threw her head back and let out a ragged scream into the night sky.

His fangs slipped out of her throat, but he was too caught up in his orgasm to notice the separation. He gave a hoarse cry of his own as he buried himself as deep inside of her as he could get and held himself there.

A few moments later, Lacy collapsed to his chest, her breathing labored. "Oh. My. God." She nipped at his ear with a giggle. "That was..."

Alex finished her sentence for her. "Amazing." A comment from that morning came back to him. "I *do* have amazing sex," he said in awe, giving a low chuckle.

"Told you," Lacy breathed, leaving a kiss against his shoulder.

He let out a soft groan of pleasure and allowed his eyes to close for a second. Once he collected himself, he opened his eyes and stared intently into hers. "I want you to do that again."

Her blue eyes clouded with confusion. "Do what again?"

Alex wrapped an arm around her waist and stood. "Orgasm." With them dripping wet, he marched purposefully toward the bedroom, never breaking the intimate connection of their lower bodies.

Lacy squealed and wrapped her legs around his waist. "You're crazy, Grimm! Again?" she cried.

"Again," he confirmed as he lowered her to the bed, finally slipping out of her. Kneeling above her, he just stared for a moment. He admired her body in the soft glow of the moonlight, reveling in each tiny detail. "Damn, you're intoxicating," he breathed. "I'm unable to resist you."

Lacy snuggled her back into the comforter and sent him an inviting look. "You're not supposed to be able to."

Resisting her was impossible. Keeping her from becoming emotionally attached to him seemed less and less likely. He was just getting himself in deeper and deeper. In more ways than one. He groaned softly at that thought. Lowering himself over her, he licked a path up her abdomen.

Lacy inhaled sharply and lifted her hips up toward him.

With a pleased grin, Alex slid his tongue upward, grazing along the underside of her left breast. He moved up once again, and with care not to puncture skin, he grazed his fangs along her nipple.

She cried out in surprise and squeezed her legs against his hips.

Alex chuckled deep in his throat as he drew her nipple into his mouth, sucking gently as he rolled the delicate bud along an extended incisor.

Once again, she arched up into him, giving a small whimper.

Watching her writhe underneath him, Alex decided he'd tortured her enough. He eased his way inside of her once again until his entire length was sheathed.

Lacy's nails dug into the flesh of his lower back as she clung to him.

He groaned softly in response, thrusting into her again and again. Her soft whimpers in his ear egged him on. He thrust harder and faster. In almost disbelief, he felt another climax approaching. He'd been doing this solely for her pleasure. He'd never expected...

He gave a hoarse cry, nearly drowning out the desperate sound of her squeak of ecstasy as they once again reached completion together. He held himself above her, frozen for a moment. Then he rolled to lie next to her.

They both stared at the ceiling, basking in the after effects of truly great sex.

It was Lacy who finally moved. She rolled over and draped herself across his chest. "Mmm," she mumbled. "I'm sleepy."

Alex froze. He wasn't used to snuggling and emotions. With only the slightest hesitation, he brushed a few strands of hair back from her face. "Let's get some rest. Tomorrow we have a busy day. I'm probably going to have to kill a few people." On Lacy's grin, he asked with amusement, "What's the smile for? Most people don't smile when they hear I'm going to have to kill people."

"You said *we*," she informed him, snuggling against his shoulder.

He smiled, dropping a spontaneous kiss to the top of her head. "I guess I did."

Chapter Five

With probably his tenth annoyed huff of the evening, Alex pounded his fist against the locked bathroom door. "I swear, if you don't come out of there this instant, I will leave you!" He hoped this threat worked better than the previous one of breaking down the door. At that, she'd merely laughed.

He honestly didn't know why he was permitting Lacy to join him to begin with. He should have just left the hotel the minute she'd turned the lock on the bathroom door. Sure, she'd have been pissed when he got back, but she would have been safe. It was going to be dangerous at the club. He was more than likely going to have to kill someone tonight. Any sane man would have put his foot down and forbidden her to tag along.

Though, truthfully, he did know why she was going. It was the sex. It had weakened his resolve and given her a power over him that no one had ever had before.

Regardless, he wasn't going to wait around forever. She'd been in the bathroom for forty minutes. He couldn't fathom what she could possibly be doing. There was nothing in the bathroom that needed forty minutes to be accomplished. He raised his fist to knock again when the door swung inward and away from his hand.

Lacy stood in the doorway. She struck a pose, showing off her outfit.

She wore the tiniest jean skirt he'd ever seen in his life. There was a small strip of black lace along the bottom that barely preserved her dignity. Above the skirt, she wore a sequin-covered, hot pink top. Glitter and sparkles covered every available inch of her shirt. At the bottom of her long legs were black, high-heeled pumps. Her skin glittered with some type of girly powder, making her shimmer. She had not a hair out of place, and her makeup was just as eye catching as her outfit. Aqua eye shadow covered her eyelids nearly to her eyebrows, and smoky, black eyeliner circled her eyes, giving her a posh raccoon effect. Mascara made her eyelashes so thick that they battled for space. Though extreme, the overall effect was enchanting. She looked good, and she knew it.

"Wow," he breathed, any annoyance he'd been feeling evaporating at the sight of her.

A grin spread across her lips at his reaction. "You look pretty 'wow' yourself." She reached out and ran a hand along his abdomen in affection as she continued. "I figured we would be playing the part of a party-hopping couple until you found the right people to kill. I wanted to look the part." Her eyes traveled upward to his hair. "The blue was ingenious. You really look like someone who parties hard."

He stifled a groan. "I did not intentionally..." He trailed off in defeat. There was no use arguing over the hair debacle. "Let's just go," he grumbled.

Lacy made a motion as if she was going to leave, but quickly skidded to a halt. "Oh! Wait. I forgot something."

He sighed. After all this time, what could she possibly still have to do? He expected her to go racing back into the bathroom, so he was filled with surprise when she suddenly grabbed both of his hands.

She lifted them and turned his palms to face outward. Stepping into him, she caused him to cup both of her breasts in his palms.

His eyebrows rose in surprise. "Um..."

A devilish grin spread across her lips. "Just giving you something to think about today."

Alex couldn't help but chuckle. He seemed to be doing that a lot where she was involved. He was unable to resist her charm. "You've already given me plenty to think about, though I don't mind the added material." To show his appreciation, he gave her breasts a quick squeeze.

When she tilted her face up to him, he lowered his head to give her a lingering kiss.

A soft murmur of approval escaped her lips before she

stepped back. She ran a finger along her bottom lip with a seductive smile before taking his hand. "We should get going. Any more of that and we'll never leave the hotel room."

Alex nodded his head in agreement. "We do need to get going." As tempting as staying in the room with her might be, they had things to do. Correction, *he* had things to do. In fact, he had a job to do, and it was time he got serious about it. Even so, he didn't argue about holding her hand.

Side by side, they left the room and entered the elevator that would take them to the lobby. They rode in silence for a moment until Lacy let out a snort of laughter.

"Something funny?" he asked with a raise of his eyebrows.

She bobbed her head in response. "Yeah. This just brings back memories."

Alex felt a flush race up his neck. "Um, yes. So you said." He sent her an apologetic look at his lack of memory.

"Let me tell you how it went," she offered. "You grabbed me and shoved me up against the wall." She giggled. "It was the wall with all the buttons. I pushed nearly all of them with my back. The two of us just rode and rode and rode...in more ways than one," she said with a wicked grin.

He cleared his throat uncomfortably as they reached the main floor and the elevator doors slid open. He was getting used to the fact that everything he'd done the night he met Lacy had been crazy and out of character. That didn't make it any less embarrassing to hear the details. "Yes...well...that was irresponsible." His protests didn't really matter. He knew that. He still felt the need to make them.

Lacy was no longer listening to him, though. She was stiff as a board as she stared out into the lobby. It appeared as if she was holding her breath, because her face was getting bright red.

"Are you alright?" he asked with concern. The red hue of her face was not at all healthy looking.

"I forgot something upstairs. We should head back up."

When she went to press the button on the wall that would take them back up to their room, he grabbed her hand to halt her. "You don't need anything but you. I'm not going back upstairs and wasting more time." He peered at her face in concern. "Are you sure you're alright? You look...spooked."

Inhaling sharply, she tightened her grip on his hand and

practically dragged him across the short space that led to the side exit. "I'm fine," she said tersely. "Let's just get out of here."

They were at the doors when a female voice called out, "Yoo-hoo! Lacy! Over here."

Lacy flinched and froze in mid-step. Closing her eyes, she took a few deep breaths before spinning around with a massive phony smile on her lips. "Bianca! I didn't see you there!"

Shooting Lacy a quick, questioning look, Alex spun to face another couple.

The woman who he assumed was Bianca pursed her lips for a moment before smiling in return. "How do you not notice your bestest friend?"

Lacy flinched again, and the skin around her eyes tightened with tension.

It was this reaction that made Alex take a closer look at the woman clopping loudly in their direction, dragging her companion along beside her.

The woman had brown hair just past her shoulders that was teased up on the sides. She was squeezed into a leopard print top that was at least two sizes too small, her breasts threatening to burst free at any moment. She was in a pair of Lycra pants that were so tight, she had to be having trouble breathing.

The man at her side had a preppy look to him. His longish blond hair was slicked back, the edges of it just barely brushing the collar of his sweater vest. His khaki pants looked as if they'd been starched, and his shoes looked freshly polished.

When she reached them, Bianca waved at Lacy, though they were less than a foot away from each other. "Hey, girlfriend!" She snapped her gum loudly as her gaze shifted to Alex. She stared at him with interest for a moment before she spun back to Lacy with a delighted look. "And who is this? You never mentioned tall, dark, and sexy here!"

Lacy took a step closer to Alex, brushing her hand self-consciously against his arm. "This is Grimm." She cleared her throat. "Alex Grimm."

"Alex," Bianca cooed. "Why have I never heard of you? Lacy should have mentioned someone as yummy as *you*."

"Can't imagine why I wouldn't," Lacy grumbled under her breath.

Bianca's eyes narrowed "What was that?"

Alex saw the flush of Lacy's cheeks and felt it was his responsibility to step up and save her. He edged forward to in-
tercept the conversation. "I'm Alex." He smiled widely, showing off his teeth in a predatory manner. "I'm Lacy's husband."

"Husband?" Bianca shrieked in astonishment. Her eyes
shot to Lacy. "Husband? I didn't even know you were seeing
someone again."

Something about this woman bothered him. She might be
Lacy's friend, but he didn't like her busybody attitude. "Well, it
was a whirlwind courtship," he said a little defensively.

"Very whirlwind," Lacy said with a forced laugh as Alex
wrapped an arm around her waist and pulled her in against
his hip.

"Besides," Alex chimed in, "it sounds like her last boyfriend was a real douche bag. It only makes sense to move
on fast and never look back."

Lacy made a strangled choking noise of surprise.

Bianca frowned, as did her companion. For a long while,
no one spoke, and an awkward silence filled the air. Finally,
Bianca broke the quiet by changing the subject. "So, Bernard's car was trashed yesterday. Looks like some idiot took
a baseball bat to it. I warned him about parking it in a public
garage, but of course he didn't listen. All types of poor people can wander their way into those things. It's really unsafe,
if you ask me." Her voice had lowered to a whisper on the
word *poor*, as if it was something to be ashamed of, something not suitable for their conversation.

Lacy shot Alex a nervous glance before quickly recovering
and spinning to the blond man with mock surprise. "No! You
love that car! How awful."

Things suddenly clicked into place for Alex. The blond in
front of them was none other than the douche bag ex-
boyfriend.

The douche bag, aka Bernard, had been looking around
with boredom until the subject of his car came up. "Hmm?"
he asked, feigning as if he had barely heard any of the conversation. "My car? Yes," he responded, voice turning stiff at
the unpleasantness of the topic. "I love that car more than
anything in the world. It was quite a pity."

Alex felt Lacy tense once again, and another uncomfortable silence followed.

Bianca repeated her attempt to start a successful conversation. "We were just here to drop off your bridesmaid dress. They arrived this morning. You're going to look beautiful at the wedding, though not as beautiful as me!" she said with a waggle of her finger.

Lacy grimaced. "No. Of course not."

Bianca gave a smug smile. "No. Of course not." She held a garment bag toward Lacy. "We tried taking this to your room, but apparently, there's been a mix up. You aren't there anymore." She pouted her full lips. "Are you having trouble, Lacy? You know you can ask me for money if you need it. We've been best friends since middle school. You can ask me for anything."

Alex's shoulders tensed at her implications, but before he could comment, Lacy did.

"Oh, there's no issue," she said brightly. She shot Bianca a superior look. "In fact," she said drawing it out, "Grimm hit the jackpot yesterday for thirty thousand dollars." She turned her attention to Alex, giving him an affectionate hug. "And we were upgraded to the honeymoon suite, free of charge. It is *amazing*."

"Very amazing," Alex agreed. He couldn't help but rub it in. "We have a hot tub in our room." He winked at Lacy suggestively.

Bianca's lips pursed. "We don't have a hot tub," she huffed in annoyance.

Bernard shrugged, his eyes on his watch. They suddenly flicked up to his fiancée, impatience in his expression. "Are we almost done with this nonsensical, female chitchat? I've got a dinner reservation."

"This late?" Lacy asked with mock innocence. "Where are you eating, a strip club?"

Bianca's eyes narrowed. "He's getting married in a few days. He's entitled to a boys' night out."

Lacy bobbed her head in agreement. "Very true. I'm sure you can trust him."

Alex heard the doubt in her voice, but either Bianca didn't or pretended not to.

"I can trust him," the brunette said haughtily.

Bernard looked at his watch again in impatience. "Sunshine," he directed at Lacy with a put upon sigh, "please don't forget to be at the chapel at six p.m. on the big day. I do know how you love to be late."

"I'll be there," Lacy said tersely.

Alex cringed at the way Bernard said *Sunshine*. He didn't think it was possible, but he hated the nickname even worse his second time hearing it, especially when coming from her ex-boyfriend. "Don't call her that," he growled.

"Well," Bernard said abruptly, completely ignoring Alex, "now that *that* is settled...if you will excuse me, I have important places to be. My life is so fulfilling and busy." He turned on his expensive shoes and marched out the door, calling over his shoulder, "Bianca, come."

Bianca rushed forward and gave Lacy an impromptu hug. "See you in a few days, honey." She looked to Alex and winked. "You too, good lookin'."

Lacy watched her friend bustle out of the building. For a full minute after they left, she stood frozen.

It was Alex who finally spoke. "Lacy?" he asked with concern.

Her eyes turned cold, and she hurried out the exit toward his car.

"Lacy!" he called out, hurrying after her. "Talk to me."

"There's nothing to talk about," she said hoarsely. She climbed into the car and roughly slammed the door.

He could tell by the rasp in her voice that she was close to tears. "Damn it," he cursed softly and climbed into the driver seat. Once he was seated, he turned to her. "Lace," he said gently.

"I'm fine," she snapped, her demeanor showing that she was indeed not fine. She shoved open the car door and slammed it again.

Alex watched in silence, unsure of what to do.

Lacy opened her door a third time. This time, when it slammed violently shut, she burst into tears. "Damn him," she sobbed. "I promised I wouldn't waste any more tears on that prick."

Alex knew talking with him would make her feel better, but it wouldn't be fun to relive her pain again. "What happened?" he pressed gently. "Your ex-boyfriend is marrying your best friend?"

"Yes." Lacy punched the glove compartment, gave a hiss of pain, and then pulled her arm back against her chest so she could cradle her injured hand. She shook it, her jaw clenched tightly as tears tracked down her cheeks.

He took her hand and held it between his own, gently stroking her now red knuckles. "Tell me about it. You'll feel better."

She sniffled and rolled her eyes. "Yeah. Sure." Using her free hand, she rubbed her eyes, smearing mascara across her cheek. "Whatever." Despite her protesting, she took a deep breath and said, "Bernard wasn't my boyfriend. He was my fiancé."

Alex tensed, unable to help himself. He just couldn't picture Lacy with that pompous jerk.

"Bernard signified everything I never had," she continued tearfully. "It wasn't the fancy yacht or the cars. It wasn't the big house." She looked glumly down at her lap. "It was the stability. Bernard offered me security. He had a family, one that loved him to death. I thought...well, I'd hoped they'd love me too." She shrugged. "That's all I wanted, somewhere to belong. But it turned out Bernard's dad was a giant pervert who wanted to love his future daughter-in-law in ways that are frowned upon."

Alex growled in anger. He couldn't believe someone would make a pass at a woman who was supposed to be like a daughter. "So you broke up with Bernard?" he asked sympathetically, noting with relief that her tears had come to a halt.

Lacy responded with a self-depreciating laugh. "No. I thought I was in love with Bernard. He was worth a little harmless sexual harassment." She sighed and let her head fall back against the headrest. Turning to face him, she said, "We broke up when I caught him fucking my best friend." She laughed again, though there was no humor in it. "He was actually the one to break things off with me. Apparently, I was being irrational and ungrateful."

Alex's eyebrows rose in incredulity, but he didn't comment. This guy was sleazier than he'd originally given him credit for.

"He told me that every man cheats. It's a fact of life. I should feel honored that he chose my best friend instead of some stranger."

Alex had to interrupt her. "Every man does not cheat. That is a load of shit."

"Is it?" she asked, looking up at him with complete vulnerability. "Maybe I'm just not sexy enough to hold a man's attention."

His eyes widened in disbelief. "Are you crazy? That jackass was insane to cheat on you. You are the sexiest woman I've met in my entire life. And I've been alive a really long time."

Lacy gave an embarrassed laugh and wiped away a few more tears from her eyes. "Really?" she asked hopefully.

Alex dropped her hand so he could cup her face in his palms. "Honey, when you appeared in my life yesterday morning out of nowhere, I about died of shock. You were the sexiest woman I'd ever laid eyes on. I couldn't figure out why you were wasting your time with me."

Lacy's eyes widened in surprise. "Are you serious? You're like, totally sexy. You are dangerous and mysterious. You're amazing in bed, and you've got abs that are insanely ripped. You are every girl's wet dream."

Alex felt blood rush to his cheeks, something that would have been impossible had he not fed the previous night. "I don't know where you get such ideas." He dropped his hands from her face in embarrassment.

Lacy practically lunged across the small console between them to wrap her arms around his neck. She pressed a kiss to his cheek. "Thank you," she whispered. "It's nice to know that Bernard is the one in the wrong and not me." She looked at the lipstick smear on his cheek and giggled. Using her thumb, she affectionately rubbed it away.

Alex wrapped an arm around her hip to pull her closer. "Like I said, the man is insane. If I would have known all this before meeting him, I would have torn his throat out right there in the lobby."

Lacy's thumb moved to his jaw, her fingers caressing the curve of his neck. "My hero."

Alex studied her for a moment. He was slightly concerned about the feelings that were suddenly coursing through him. They were warm and fuzzy. These feelings frightened him more than the lust. Lust faded. This...this felt much more dangerous.

Pushing his own worries aside, he asked, "Why are you

still friends with Bianca? You should be screaming and pulling hair. This deserves a catfight. I don't think there is anyone out there who would blame you."

Lacy shrugged and leaned her head against his shoulder. "I don't know. Everything just caught me by surprise. She stopped by my shitty little apartment a few weeks later. I assumed she was there to apologize. Instead, she tells me that we are far too good of friends to let a man get between us. She acted like everything was perfectly fine. I was so stunned I didn't know what to do." She shook her head against his shoulder as if she still couldn't believe it. "Four months later, she asks me to be her maid of honor. When I informed her that four months seemed like they were rushing things, she told me they'd been seeing each other for over sixteen months." Lacy's head lifted from his shoulder as anger once again filled her. "Sixteen months! They'd been screwing behind my back for over a year! He was fucking her before we got engaged!"

Alex watched her shoulders rise and fall in rapid succession with her frantic breathing. Before he could question what he was doing, he grabbed her firmly by the shoulders. Lowering his mouth to hers, he kissed her roughly.

Lacy gave a squeak of surprise, but responded, sliding her hands along his forearms.

Alex pulled back, staring deep into her eyes. "I will never do that to you. Bernard was a fool, and your friend is a clueless airhead. Neither of them deserves you in their lives."

Lacy smiled at him, her blue eyes going soft with emotion. "You're too good to me. A wet dream with a sensitive side. How'd I get so lucky?"

He squeezed her shoulders with a grin. "Just wait. I'll be driving you crazy within a week."

She rolled her eyes. "Whatever." Sliding back into her seat, she looked up at him in amusement. "You know what else would make me feel good?"

His eyebrows rose at her blunt question. "What's that?"

"Take me dancing. Let's go to this club, kick some vampire ass, and have a good time of it."

A wide grin spread across his lips at her request. Turning the engine over, he threw the car into drive. "I like the way you think." He frowned as he pictured himself on a crowded dance floor. "At least about the kicking ass part."

"Killing people you are cool with, but the thought of danc-ing freaks you out." Lacy studied him for a moment while he peeled out of the parking lot and onto the busy street. Final-ly, she broke into laughter. "You are such a vampire!"

Chapter Six

In less than ten minutes time at the Nocturnal Lady, Alex was involved in a brutal fight to the death. Upon entering the club, he had guided Lacy to the bar so he could scope out the building.

She'd ordered two vodkas, sliding one to him along the short distance of bar that separated them. "Brings back memories, huh?" She rolled her eyes with a chuckle. "Or maybe in your case, it doesn't." She shrugged in amusement as she swirled the contents around in her glass. "Drink up," she said with a wink. "I doubt it can result in anything weirder than last time."

"I sure hope not," Alex grunted with a voice low and gravely.

They'd both downed their drinks together and slammed the empty glasses back down to the bar simultaneously.

He'd felt the liquid burn its way down his throat. It was like drinking liquid sunlight. "I hate vodka," he'd complained with a grimace.

With her face flushed from the alcohol, Lacy agreed. After that, they decided to stay away from the vodka. It made them do crazy things.

Lacy had turned to him and asked him to take her out on the dance floor.

Before he could even begin to protest, he'd been grabbed from behind and thrown with inhuman strength toward the dance floor.

That is where he was now, staring up at the ceiling of the Nocturnal Lady and wincing at the pain shooting up his spine

from hitting the unforgiving tile. With a groan, he hefted himself off the ground to face his attacker. He saw Lacy's blue
eyes widen in surprise, but didn't have time to reassure her
that he was perfectly fine before a boot was kicked into his
gut. He stumbled backwards onto the dance floor, but finally
managed to get a good look at his attacker.

The fangs protruding from the man's mouth were a dead
giveaway that he was a vampire. His shirt was a ghastly orange and brown swirl of a mess that reminded Alex of vomit.
His pants were brown corduroy with belled bottoms.

"A vampire trapped in the seventies," Alex observed dryly. "Not cool."

Lacy, who had raced to the edge of the dance floor during his attack, giggled at this, seemingly recovered from her
initial shock.

He frowned in response. He'd been spending too much
time with this little vixen. When had he ever even noticed an
enemy's outfit before, let alone commented on it? He didn't
do witty banter. He fought. He killed. He went about his day.

While he was distracted by these thoughts, the vampire
in 70s apparel aimed a kick at his ribs.

Alex jumped to the side. He avoided the majority of the
blow, the vampire's heeled boot grazing his midsection.

Lacy watched with interest as he ducked a punch aimed
at his jaw. "You need help, baby?"

Alex yanked a stake from his back pocket, flipping it so
the thick end rested in his palm. When the other man
charged him, Alex took him by surprise by jamming the
stake deep into the vampire's chest. He watched the vampire
turn to dust with grim satisfaction, then spun to Lacy. "No. I
don't need help. Like you would know what to do with a
vampire."

Lacy shrugged, unconcerned.

Alex sighed, but couldn't stop his lip from twitching in
amusement as it threatened a smile. "Thank you anyway."
He glanced around them. Seeing at least two more vampires
approaching, he quickly returned his gaze to her. "I've gotten
their attention. Things are probably about to get very violent," he hollered to her over the still pumping music. "You
should get somewhere safe."

Lacy nodded. "I absolutely agree. Somewhere safe."

To his amazement, she took five steps away from him and struck a sexy pose. Her foot started tapping, and then her head started bobbing. A moment later, her hips started swaying.

His jaw dropped in disbelief as she started dancing, her body gyrating to the music that pounded through the speakers that surrounded the room. "Lacy," he chastised, "I said somewhere safe!"

She gave him a playful wink and turned her back on him. Her hands lifted above her head, her fists pumping the air in time to the beat of a song he'd never heard before.

"I cannot believe—" Alex's complaints were cut short by a fist colliding with his nose. He grunted in pain, his hand moving to cover his bleeding face as he reeled backwards. "Damn it," he growled. "That wasn't fair." A stupid comment, he knew. Criminals never played fair, and vampires were even worse than humans.

A massive beast of a man stood grinning at him, his mouth looking like a Jack-o-lantern from hell due to his few randomly placed teeth. "I'll give you more warning next time." His grin widened as he nodded behind Alex. "Here comes my friend."

Alex spun in just enough time to get a fist to the gut. He hunched over, a grunt of pain escaping him. When the undead Jack-o-lantern came around to leer in his face, Alex cringed. "First, I have to kill a vampire from the seventies. Now, I get attacked by a redneck, hillbilly bloodsucker. Vegas really is the place for freak shows."

Inhaling deeply, Alex assessed the damage done to his ribs. Sharp pain didn't shoot through his body, meaning none seemed to be broken. "You've barely got any teeth. Seriously, how do you manage to drink like that? You've only got one fang. It can't be easy sinking that into someone's throat. That's like having one ball. It's emasculating."

Alex couldn't ever remember a time when he'd talked this much during a fight. It seemed to be working nicely, though, because the Jack-o-lantern was looking infuriated, thus sloppy, as people tended to be when they let their emotions get the better of them.

This point was proven when pumpkin head gave a roar of outrage.

The noise was loud, but only a few people on the dance floor even bothered to glance in their direction. The music was just too loud to notice anything else, and humans were just too damn oblivious to anything supernatural going on around them. The drunken idiot they would notice immediately and scorn, but rabid vampires didn't pop up on their radar. It was an extreme case of selective attention.

The Jack-o-lantern snarled in the direction of the human dancers who were no longer paying attention before returning his glare to Alex. He gave a battle cry and lunged toward Alex's midsection.

Prepared for this assault, Alex caught the gap-toothed vampire by the back of his shirt, then lifted his knee into the other man's jaw. He heard the satisfying sound of bone breaking and idly wondered if he'd managed to knock out any of the few remaining teeth in the man's head. He didn't have time to relish this small victory, though, because the Jack-o-lantern's friend, who was also in need of a visit to the dental hygienist, jumped into the fray.

Alex dodged a shot to his ribs from the newest vampire and, in the same movement, brought his fist into the vampire's face with enough force to break the skin on his knuckles. His other hand, which was still grasping the stake, slammed upward into the vampire's chest. He felt the stake slide through skin and meat, tearing muscle as it found its way to the heart. He hadn't even had time to think of a clever name for the Jack-o-lantern's friend, and already, he was dead.

He smirked arrogantly as the vampire disintegrated into ash. Taking a step back, he shook his aching left hand and inspected the damage. Blood caked his knuckles. Some of it was his. Most was not. He idly thought that it was a good thing vampires didn't have to worry about things such as blood-borne pathogens. "There goes that manicure," he observed, rubbing a smudge of blood from his thumbnail.

He quickly forgot about his nails as Lacy danced across his field of vision. With a growl, he took a step in her direction. "Lacy, I thought I said—" Once again, he was hit while distracted, this time taking a shot to the kidneys from behind that nearly dropped him to his knees. He groaned as pain raced through his back. He was about to turn and face his attacker when he noticed another vampire just to his left.

This vampire marched past him, moving purposefully in Lacy's direction.

Alex barely managed to grab the newest vampire by the collar of his jacket and yank him backwards.

This vampire, a blond who looked better suited for *GQ* than a nightclub brawl, went bowling into his co-worker.

Caught off guard by the unexpected weight, the Jack-o-lantern collapsed to the ground.

While both of them struggled to get to their feet, Alex silently wished for a can of gasoline and a match. It had been a long time since he'd been to a bonfire. With a sigh at having to dispose of them by hand, he pulled a stake made from the end of a table leg from a low pocket on the back of his pants. He kept a stake in each hand as he approached the pair.

As both vampires got to their feet, Alex was ready. He flung the pieces of wood with inhuman force. Both struck their intended targets.

Simultaneously, the vampires' eyes widened in surprise. In the next instant, they were both dust.

The stakes clattered to the floor, followed by the ashy remains of the vampires, but Alex was already too busy looking for his next adversary to notice. He spun in a circle, searching the darkened room and crowd for any more hostile, undead bouncers, but there were none. The closest hostile thing was a woman shooting him a look of annoyance after she stumbled on one of the fallen stakes.

Once he was sure things were safe, Alex spun to Lacy.

She was staring at him with an expression he could only describe as desire. Her bottom lip was caught between her teeth, and she seemed to be fighting back a grin.

As he approached her, he couldn't keep the surprise off his face at her odd reaction to his murderous battle. "Um...so..."

Her arms were around his neck before he could even think of something else to say. "Grimm, that was breathtaking. You are a total badass. You weren't lying about keeping weapons on you." Her hands slid along his waist, her expression pensive. Her fingertips brushed along the gun he kept at his back in the waistband of his pants. "You've got a gun?"

she squealed in delight. "Damn. That is so...sexy."

Alex tried very politely to remove her hands from him, suddenly wishing he'd remembered his holster, which was in his office back home. He couldn't fathom how it was sexy to sneak a gun into a nightclub. "So, the bouncers are all dead. The owner probably has security cameras he witnessed this all on, but on the off chance that he doesn't, I would like to get to the back offices before he realizes what's going on." His eyes roved over her, his expression one of skepticism. "Will you be okay here on your own?"

Lacy slid away from him and jerked a thumb toward the DJ. "Are you kidding? I love this song!"

He tried very hard to keep his temper from rearing its ugly head. "Lacy, this isn't..." He trailed off. This was a losing battle. He couldn't explain to her that this wasn't a social visit, that it wasn't meant to be fun. Everything seemed to be fun to her, even killing. He gave a sigh of resignation. "Just be careful, okay?"

She nodded, waving him off. "Always. Besides, if I'm not, I've always got you to keep me safe."

Alex had been about to walk away in satisfaction until the second sentence sunk in. With a huff, he spun back around to face her. "Lacy," he growled in warning, but she was no longer there.

She was halfway across the dance floor, jamming like there wasn't the slightest threat to her health.

He shook his head with a sigh. "Please be careful," he whispered under his breath. With one last concerned look, he turned and headed toward a darkened hallway at the back of the club. He'd been scoping that area out before he'd been rudely attacked.

It was the most likely place for an office. His money was on the Bear being back there, hopefully too distracted with counting his blood money to notice any disturbances.

As much as he hated to, Alex pushed Lacy to the back of his thoughts. She was a big girl. She could look out for herself while he took care of the bad guys. As he headed into the darkened hallway, he glanced over his shoulder to see if anyone was following him.

No one even glanced in his direction. Everyone was too busy downing shots, trying to attract members of the opposite sex, or dancing. Most were doing a combination of all of these things.

Shaking his head at how clueless humans were to their surroundings, he entered the hall. It was dark and uninviting, probably a ploy to make everyday clubbers hesitate. It didn't bother Alex. He had excellent night vision. He could see well enough.

He passed up a storage room and what appeared to be an employee bathroom. The last door in the hall had a *Do Not Enter* sign in bold letters across the center. "I believe I've found what I am looking for," Alex said under his breath. He searched next to the door and was happy not to find a code lock. There was really no need to have coded locks and reinforced doors when the people you were screwing over were only human.

Taking a deep breath, he wrapped his hand around the doorknob and turned it. The door eased open without any resistance, revealing a short man whose back was to the door.

Hearing someone enter his office, the man swiveled toward Alex. It appeared as if he'd been turned into a vampire in his mid-forties. His hair was thinning, but what was left of it was slicked back. He was slightly overweight, his gut hanging over his belt.

Alex cringed. The man was forever trapped in the state of unkempt slob. It would be depressing enough to turn nearly anyone to a life of crime. "Walter," he greeted enthusiastically.

The man's brow furrowed. "Do I know you?"

Alex held out a hand. "One of your men sent me back. Blond guy, real pretty face."

"David," Walter hissed in agitation. "That's against club protocol. He knows that. He is so dead." He slid his sausage-thick fingers into Alex's for a handshake, his expression curious.

As soon as Alex got a grip on the other man's hand, he tightened it. He clenched until he felt the other vampire's bones grind together. "He *is* dead," he agreed, "and I'm the one who killed him."

Walter's eyes widened when he realized what was happening. "What do you want?" he seethed, though fear showed through his outrage.

Alex yanked on Walter's arm, drawing him closer and causing his legs to bang against his desk. "I want some information about your boss. I know he's been sending you around to threaten local businesses. I would put my money on him having you do more than that. I would bet you've been sending him girls too, girls looking for a little gambling money who are too dumb to realize what they're getting themselves into. You're pimping blood for him. You know those girls get in way over their heads and wind up dead."

"I don't know what you're talking about," Walter lied nervously.

In one swift movement, Alex slammed Walter's face down onto the surface of the desk. "Wrack your tiny little brain. Did you send him a woman named Darlie?"

An evil chuckle escaped Walter, and he spat blood onto the desktop. "Now I remember. Pretty redhead? Cute little ass? They did her good, didn't they?" he taunted. "I hear that David had his way with her while the rest drained her dry."

Alex growled, suddenly wishing he'd made David suffer a little more before killing him. "Who's your boss?" he growled, barely keeping himself from going into a violent rage.

"My boss is a very dangerous man. You push him, and he will kill everyone you care about."

Alex's thoughts immediately went to Lacy, and he lunged across the desk, driving his fist into Walter's face.

Blood spurted from the Bear's nose, and he gave a hiss of aggravation. "Touch a nerve, did I?"

His hands fisting into Walter's shirt, Alex spun the other man, dragging him over the top of the desk, and slamming him up against the wall. "Who the fuck do you work for?" he snarled.

"The devil," Walter responded flippantly. "He wants you to join him in hell."

Alex grabbed a stake from his pocket and drove it toward Walter's heart, stopping an inch from his shirt. "Tell me, or I will end you."

Walter's eyes lowered warily to the stake. He finally seemed to be taking Alex's threats seriously, because in a trembling voice, he said, "I only send the girls his way. I've never killed any of them personally."

Alex's fingers tightened on the stake, his knuckles turning

white from the strain. "Where do you send them to? And who does the dirty work? Surely not the head guy himself."

Walter's eyes were wide with fear, and he kept glancing toward the door as if waiting for help. None would be coming. Alex had killed them all. "I think the head guy joins in sometimes. I guess he misses the fear of a fresh kill. He likes to hear the screams." On the angered look he received, Walter rushed to continue. "They use some of my men occasionally. They don't like to use the same guys every time. They don't want to leave a traceable pattern. Cops might start to notice girls disappearing with the same men before their bodies turn up. They do...did like to use Dave a lot, though. He was a good-looking guy. Women usually let their guards down around him. It made suckering them in easier."

Alex pulled Walter away from the wall slightly and then slammed him back against it hard enough to crack the drywall. "Where do you send them?"

"He'll kill me if I tell."

"I'll kill you if you don't," Alex threatened, "and I won't be half as merciful."

Walter made a noise that sounded close to a sob. "Alright! Alright! He tells me to send them to the big track where they race all those horses. You know the one I mean, right? It's the track next to the hotel on the main drag that has all the sand and fake palm trees. I think it's supposed to be a beach theme or something. He meets the girls there and offers them whatever it is they want for what they think is a ridiculously low recompense in return. Only they don't realize they're offering up their lives as payment. They think he's some nut job from a blood bank or something looking to reel in extra donors."

"How do I know who your boss is? You've got to give me more than that," Alex growled.

"I'm getting to that," Walter cried with a strangled yelp. "He sits in section D, seat twenty-two. He said he's there every Thursday night after dark. He'll be wearing a hat and shades."

"Sunglasses? At night? Really?" Alex asked in disgust. "Could he be more conspicuous?" His eyes narrowed threateningly. "Are you lying to me?"

Walter squirmed in Alex's grip. "No, man! I swear! That's

all I know!"

Alex suddenly released him. Dusting Walter's jacket off, he said, "You've been quite the help." He smoothed Walter's collar, mocking intimate camaraderie. "I really do appreciate this."

Walter gave a nervous smile. "Y...you're welcome."

Alex beamed, showing off razor sharp fangs. "I'll tell your boss the Bear says *hi*." As Walter's eyes widened in horror at the thought of his boss discovering who ratted him out, Alex pulled back and shoved the stake into the vampire's chest.

Alex stared the other man in the eyes as he jammed the jagged wood into a heart that hadn't been beating for decades. "Don't worry about your boss," he said as Walter disintegrated into dust. "You won't be around to have to worry about his revenge." With that, he turned and left the office.

Chapter Seven

Alex stomped toward the dance floor in agitation, searching for Lacy. Now that the imminent danger was over, he was riled up over the fact that she hadn't run when things turned violent. He'd demanded she run, yet still she'd stayed. She was impossible. Once he found her, he was going to strangle her...or at least give her a serious scolding.

With his temper flaring, he stamped through the thronging, sweaty bodies that gyrated on the black and white linoleum tiles serving as a dance floor. His jaw dropped in disbelief when his eyes finally landed on Lacy.

Lacy, his *wife*, was on top of the bar, shaking her ass for the entire club to see. She was clinging to the arm of some preppy shmuck and laughing in delight as she sloshed beer over the rim of the mug in her hand.

The guy's arm was around her waist, and before Alex's eyes, he pulled her closer. The man's hand slid lower, cupping Lacy's ass and pulling the front of her body against his.

Lacy winked at the man before shimmying out of his grip. She raised her glass of beer above her head and gave out a whoop of enjoyment, which the crowd below echoed. Her free arm wrapped around the man's neck, and she once again let him wrap his arms around her waist. She let him rub her against the crotch of his pants, let his hands paw at her body.

Alex knew jealousy was an irrational, human emotion, but that didn't stop it from rearing up inside of him. He marched purposefully over to the bar and yanked his wife down from the countertop, his hand wrapped completely around her upper arm. "What was that?" he demanded, motioning toward the bar and the stranger she'd been practically hanging all over.

The man she'd been dancing with opened his mouth to protest his dance partner being yanked away, but Alex silenced him with a glare.

"What was *what*?" Lacy asked, shaking her arm free of his grip.

Alex once again waved toward the bar. "This," he said shortly. "You." His expression turned even angrier. "I wanted you to get somewhere safe. What exactly were you thinking?" As a last thought, he added, "And who the *fuck* was that guy?"

Lacy went to answer, but faltered at his last question. "Him?" she asked in confusion. "Just some guy." She brushed her hair away from her eyes. "You said when we got here that you wanted us to blend in. I figured the best way to do that was to dance like I had a ton of baggage I wanted to unload on the dance floor, which I suppose I kind of did. I danced away my frustrations over Bernard. I'm actually sort of horny now." She gave him an encouraging smile. "Plus, someone's going to notice if a vampire suddenly kills the life of the party. And these guys don't want to draw attention to themselves. While I was up on that bar, I was sort of untouchable. Plus, I figured you would keep me safe." She pinched his cheek playfully. "I trust you."

Alex opened his mouth to argue, but couldn't find anything to complain about. She had a good point. The best way to blend in was to do what she'd done, and no vampire was going to risk hurting her when she was so publicly visible. She'd actually probably picked the safest place in the entire bar. As he frowned over how much sense her logic made, the music suddenly switched to a slow tempo.

Lacy stared up at him through the sparkles shot through the air by a large disco ball. "You're not mad, are you?" She stepped closer. "You'll still dance with me, right?"

Alex sighed in resignation. "No. I'm not mad." Her second question was much harder to answer. "I...I'm...well, dancing...it..." He made a face. "I'm not exactly..."

With an affectionate grin, Lacy slid her arms around his neck. "I've got you covered, big boy. I'll lead."

He couldn't help but give her a soft grin in return. "That would be helpful." Giving in, he curved his arms around her waist and pulled her close. "You drive me crazy, Lace. You know that, right?" He sighed, relaxing in response to the calming music and the feel of her fingers sliding through the hair at the back of his neck. "I worry about you," he confided, as if it was a character flaw.

"You don't have to worry so much," she chastised. "I can handle myself, you know?" She smirked and arched an eyebrow. "I even had to stake a vampire while you were gone."

Alex felt his heart plummet to his toes. "*What*?" he cried loudly. He noticed a few questioning looks from nearby couples, so he lowered his voice and whispered, "What?"

Lacy shrugged casually, though her expression was one of complete pride. "You left one."

"And...and you killed it?" he asked in disbelief. "How?"

An adorable pout jutted her bottom lip out. "How? I just did what I saw you do, piece of jagged wood to the heart."

"I didn't even think you were paying attention," he admitted.

"Well I was just pretending not to as part of the facade." She stepped in closer to him and leaned her head on his shoulder. "Now could we please get to the romantic part of the evening?"

Alex grinned at the top of her head. "I didn't realize there was supposed to be a romantic part of the evening. I thought this was all about death and mayhem." As he said this, his arms tightened around her, and he nuzzled the hair next to her ear.

Lacy smiled against the soft cotton of his shirt. "We're newlyweds. Everything is the romantic part. We've got a little death and mayhem going on the side is all."

"I see," Alex said with a chuckle in response. "Then by all means, let me romance you." His lips traveled down to press a kiss against her ear. He then caressed a kiss along her jawline. "Is this better?" he breathed against the soft skin of her throat.

"Much," Lacy whispered with a giggle. She slid her hands from his neck to his cheeks. She forced him to look her in the eyes for a moment. Then she stood on her tiptoes and kissed him.

Alex growled deep in his throat and tightened his hold on her waist. He knew he shouldn't be leading her on like this, but it seemed he kept doing so against his better judgment. Even if it was only for a few minutes at a time, it was nice to do something almost normal.

He knew it was going to kill him when this whole happy bubble burst, but he was going to enjoy it for now. He deepened the kiss, nudging her mouth open with his. He'd never been one for displays of affection, let alone ones in public.

Lacy was making him do all kinds of things he wouldn't normally do. Hell, if he could have sex in an elevator, he could surely steal a few kisses on the dance floor.

He was just sliding his hands over her backside when someone cleared their throat at his elbow.

Lacy spun immediately to face the person, but it took his sluggish brain a moment to comprehend the interruption and turn to face the intruder. The woman standing before them made his breath catch in his throat and his stomach somersault with anxiety. "Regina," he gasped in surprise.

Lacy's eyebrows shot nearly to her hairline. "Regina," she repeated almost accusingly. Her eyes flicked back and forth between the two of them, narrowing at the awkward silence that followed. "You know each other," she stated, catching on quickly.

"You could say that." Regina responded in her low, velvety voice as an amused smile crept up her lips.

Alex stared at Regina, feeling as helpless as if he was facing down the rising of the sun. Gorgeous she might be, but her appearance right now would lead nowhere good; he was certain of it. Had she arrived a few days earlier...or perhaps a few days later once he'd sorted out the situation with Lacy... He studied Regina with apprehension.

Her long black hair was done in loose curls nearly to her waist. Her large, almond-colored eyes were surrounded by dark, smoky eye shadow. Eyeliner and mascara brought her features out, giving her an exotic appearance. She looked even more stunning since the last time he'd seen her.

Regina put a hand on her hip and cocked it, bringing his attention to her outfit.

She wore black leather pants and matching work boots. A gray sweater did nothing to lighten her appearance. It only made her all the more intimidating.

"You could definitely say that," he whispered breathlessly, afraid to speak any louder. Besides, she could hear him over the loud music with her vampiric hearing, and Lacy was close enough to him to hear the softest whisper.

Lacy. His gaze swept to her. He studied her sun-kissed blonde hair, her hot pink, sequined top. His eyes flicked between Regina and Lacy. They were like night and day. He couldn't envision two people more different, which made the situation all the more difficult.

Realizing they'd been standing in silence for longer than was probably socially acceptable, Alex forced his voice to work. "Regina, this is Lacy. Lacy, Regina." At a close inspection of Lacy's eyes, he could read jealousy. He quickly reassured her by adding, "Regina is my sister." He saw realization hit her eyes a moment before they widened.

"Your...sister." Lacy gave Regina an appraising look while the other woman did the same in return.

Alex shot his sister a pleading look, silently begging her to be nice. She was older than him by three years and never let him forget it. She enjoyed nothing more than harassing him and making him feel like a bumbling imbecile. He did not wish for such treatment to be given to Lacy.

Regina's eyes widened in shock as if she couldn't understand the warning glare sent her way. After a look of innocence for his benefit, she spun to Lacy. "Sweetie, we have got to sit down and have a chat. Apparently, Alex wasn't totally forthcoming in his desperate text message for help."

"Desperate text message," Alex grumbled in protest. Sure, he'd sent his sister a simple message asking for some assistance if she was available, but it was hardly desperate. That had also been before Darlie was murdered. Her showing up now was most inconvenient.

Lacy giggled as Regina took her elbow and led her to a table in a dark, quiet corner. "Vampires who text message, that's too funny."

Regina patted Lacy's arm, then slid into a seat at the table. "We do all kinds of things. We send text messages. We participate in oral sex. We play video games. We smoke weed. We're into modern stuff just as much as humans."

Alex gave a sharp intake of air in offense as he took the seat next to Lacy. "I do *not* smoke weed."

"Oh," Regina said flippantly. She took a compact out of her pocket and checked her lipstick. "That's just me."

While Alex's face was turning red, Regina's lips slid into a wicked grin. She eyed Alex over the compact mirror. "So you are admitting that you enjoy oral sex?"

Alex felt his cheeks flush even redder. The amusement on Lacy's face made it all the more embarrassing. "Regina," he practically growled. "I do *not—*"

His sister snapped her compact closed and held up a hand. "Please, little brother. I don't want to know." She spun to Lacy and leaned forward to loudly mock whisper. "He hasn't been on a date in over two hundred years. Two hundred years! And then it was only because I forced him to come along on a double date with a werewolf friend of mine." Regina flopped back in her seat with a put upon huff. "Now here he is with blue hair, making out in public. What have you done to my little brother?"

Instead of being embarrassed, Lacy looked pleased. She lounged back in her seat and kicked her long legs up on the chair across from her. "Two hundred years? That's adorable!"

As both women grinned at him, a horrible realization hit Alex. Lacy wasn't intimidated by his sister like everyone else on the planet. They actually seemed to be...getting along. He'd thought it was nearly impossible for another woman to be around Regina for any period of time without wanting to rip her hair out. Now he realized it was much worse than the two of them going at each other like rabid animals. They were bonding over his humiliation. The two of them were going to get along peachy keen, because they both took sick pleasure in watching him squirm.

"You should have seen him on that date," Regina confided. "He was all bumbling and awkward. I can't imagine how he caught the affections of a beautiful woman such as yourself." A look of morbid fascination crossed her face. "He didn't go all caveman, did he? Bash you over the head and drag you to his hotel room? I've seen my brother fight. He can be quite scary when there's something he desires."

Lacy let out peals of laughter. "No. He didn't bash me over the head."

"Good," Regina breathed with exaggerated relief. "I was worried. Someone with that much bottled up sexual tension is just a disaster waiting to happen."

"Now wait just a minute," Alex growled. Sure, he didn't date nearly as much as his big sister, but he'd had fleeting relationships in the past.

His anger only made the girls titter. Lacy wiped a tear of laughter from her eye and said, "You can rest assured, he didn't do anything violent. All it takes to get your brother to unwind is a lot of vodka. You get him to slip once and do something fun, then he becomes like a wild, untamed animal."

Regina sucked in an over-exaggerated gasp. "He was drinking?" She spun to Alex. "You were *drinking*?"

He rolled his eyes and absentmindedly stroked Lacy's elbow. "Enough already." He sent Regina a pointed glare. "A woman is dead. I sent you a message because I thought you could help, not because I wanted to sit around and listen to you mock me." He ran a hand miserably along the back of his neck. He'd contacted Regina the moment he realized he was in over his head. He was a damn fine private detective, but he was going up against an entire crime organization, not just a single perpetrator. He'd enlisted help as soon as he could; only it hadn't been soon enough. "Too bad I couldn't keep her alive long enough for you to get here."

"That sounds more like my brother," Regina said grimly as she sat up at attention in her chair. "I'm sorry, Alex. I didn't realize..." She sent him an apologetic look. "I'll chit-chat with your girlfriend later. Right now, we can get down to work."

The mood was suddenly grim, but Lacy mumbled out, "Wife."

Regina's mouth was open, but she froze on whatever she'd been about to say. Though her body never moved, her eyes flicked to Lacy. "What did you say?"

"Wife," Lacy repeated. "I'm his wife."

Regina's hand slapped loudly to the tabletop, causing Alex to wince. "Wait! *What*?" She looked between the two of them, her eyes wide. "Forget the dead girl! Sorry, Alex, but she ain't getting any deader." She lifted a hand up and waved it dramatically in the air. "Back up. Explain. *Married*?"

Alex could feel his face flushing once again. He'd been dead and on his own for a few hundred years, but his sister still had the ability to make him blush. "It isn't a big deal."

"It *is* a big deal! My little brother gets married, and I wasn't even there to see it."

"It was a drunken mistake," he grumbled, trying to change the subject from his love life.

Lacy elbowed him roughly in the side. "A mistake we're both realizing we're glad we made."

Regina sent her brother a glare for his callous comment before turning to Lacy. "Please tell me he's consummated the marriage. He can be such a prude, and with an attitude like that..."

Lacy giggled. "No worries. He definitely consummated."

Alex groaned and covered his face with his hands. "Are you done?" he asked. "Can we move on from the 'demean Alex' portion of the conversation?"

Lacy shot Regina a wide grin before patting Alex on the knee. "Of course, baby. Let's talk about the dead girl."

He grumbled in response, but was relieved that the girls were finally ready to get down to business. Yet before he could even start to catch Regina up on the case, Lacy interrupted him. "Hey!" She cried out with an almost urgent tone in her voice and turned her curious gaze to Regina. "Something just occurred to me... How did you know to find us here? Did you use some sort of crazy vampire power? Are you linked to Alex mentally? Are you, like, honed in to his position?" Her eyes were wide and full of excited wonder. "Are you *psychic*?"

Regina gave a snort of amusement and shook her head. "I tracked the GPS on his cell phone," she supplied almost apologetically.

"Oh..." Lacy's expression was one of disappointment. "Such a human thing to do. Bummer." With a disenchanted shake of her head, she turned back to Alex. "Well...since that was a total letdown, on with the case, I suppose."

He arched a brow, but chose not to comment. Instead, he filled his sister in on everything that had happened involving the case with Darlie up until this point.

Regina listened intently, bobbing her head slightly in agreement at certain details. "So I take it you want me to go undercover?" she finally asked.

"Originally, that was the plan. I—"

"I could have always gone undercover," Lacy said with a pout.

Regina shook her head in disagreement. "Not like me, honey. He wants me to get in with the men who are killing these girls. He wants an inside source, and they aren't going to welcome in anyone who isn't a vampire."

Alex nodded in confirmation. "That is what I wanted in the beginning, but I'm not sure I do anymore. Lacy got us a good lead, and things have been unfolding since then. It doesn't make sense at this point to put you in danger by having you go undercover."

Regina sighed. "You don't see the whole picture, darling. When the final battle goes down, and you know it will, you're going to want someone with you. If I'm undercover, I'll be on the inside already. It's safer all around that way. If we're lucky, I'll get you some extra intel. At the very least, I can try to get surviving hostages to safety while you battle it out."

He opened his mouth to speak, but she interrupted him. "You know it makes sense. Don't argue because your over-protective brother gene is acting up. You know I can hold my own in a fight, or you wouldn't have called me. You know you could use my help."

Alex felt his jaw twitch as he ground his teeth together, but finally, he conceded. "Fine. Just promise me that if you think for even a second they might be on to you, you'll get out of there."

"Deal," she chirped. "Now...I need you to give me at least a day. Let me meet with the next guy on your list before you kill him. I'll tell him I worked for Walter, that I think someone is after us. If I can worm my way in and earn his trust, you may be able to skip over him altogether. You can head straight to the main source."

"He dies for his involvement," Alex growled.

Regina shot him a worried glance. "Damn. Someone needs some anger management." After a moment, she re-lented. "Fine. He dies for his involvement. You can torture him all you want. *After* he lets me talk to the man in charge. Understood?"

Alex growled something unintelligible.

"*Understood?*" On his grudging nod, Regina added, "You need a night off anyway. Go take it easy and act like the newlywed you are. Have a night filled with champagne and kinky sex."

"I don't—"

Regina cut him off. "I don't want to know! Just go do it!" Her eyes narrowed. "That's an order, young man!"

Chapter Eight

"She drives me insane," Alex growled about his sister as he climbed into his car and slammed the door shut behind him. "She treats me like a child! I've been alive over four hundred years! I don't need her meddling in my personal life."

Lacy bit her upper lip with a smirk. "I don't know. I kinda liked her."

He shot her a dark look. "Of course you did. The two of you ganged up on me. I felt like I was in front of a firing squad. Blindfolded. With my hands tied behind my back."

"Was it as bad as all that?" she asked with a giggle.

"Worse," he said, shooting a glance her way as he started the car and eased onto the road.

Lacy waved him off. "I think it's cute. You're as old as dirt and you still squabble with your sister. It makes you seem almost normal."

"It's not cute," he argued. "I'm a vampire. I am not cute!"

"Okay. Okay," Lacy said unconvincingly. "You're not cute. You're fearsome and dangerous. I'm shaking in my designer boots." Her lack of a quavering voice made her concession ring false. So did her flippant, casual air as she leaned forward and flicked on the radio.

Alex's grip tightened on the wheel as she flipped through stations. Music, sports broadcasters, and DJs blared through the speakers, changing so quickly it was impossible to discern one from the other.

Finally, just when he thought he might drive them both into the Grand Canyon, she settled on a station. "I love this song!" She yanked the dial to turn the sound up by five decibels.

"Really?" he commented dryly. "Because it sounds like just a bunch of obnoxious noise to me."

"Come on," Lacy pleaded. "Don't be so...*old*."

Alex rolled his eyes as he made a left turn onto the main strip of Vegas, heading toward their hotel. He stayed silent, lost in his own thoughts about the case.

While he did this, Lacy danced in her seat, thoroughly enjoying the trashy story of a girlfriend who was a dick magnet. The top was down in the convertible, so she inched up in her seat until she was practically standing. She lifted her hands above her head with a whoop of enjoyment, then hollered the words along with the musician.

Alex glimpsed at her, relenting with a small smile at her enthusiasm. When he turned his eyes back to the road, it took his brain a moment to register that her shirt had slid up, exposing her stomach. He glanced back over.

Her skirt was so low on her waist that he could see her hipbone jutting out. Her bellybutton ring gleamed tantalizingly at him. Her stomach was at eye level, and all he wanted to do at that moment was lean over and kiss his way across her exposed flesh.

It was then that he realized he was no longer paying attention to the road. His gaze rushed back to the pavement stretching in front of him only to realize he'd drifted partially onto the shoulder. He yanked the wheel quickly, jerking them back into proper place.

An instant later, sirens sounded in the air. Glancing in his rearview mirror, Alex saw the flashing lights of a police cruiser. "Shit," he cursed. "This is your fault," he grumbled to Lacy.

Her eyes widened in surprise as she slid down in her seat, quickly fastening her seatbelt. "My fault?"

Alex grumbled something about her skirt under his breath that even he didn't understand as he put the car in park and cranked off the radio.

Lacy craned her neck behind them to look at the squad car. "Oh crap. Oh crap. Oh crap," she repeated over and over again in a nervous voice. She chewed on a fingernail while her blue eyes darted about as if looking for an escape. "What are we going to do?" she fretted. "We're screwed. We're going to jail."

Alex shot her a puzzled look as he calmly grabbed his wallet. "And why are we in all this trouble?"

"You don't have a license," she hissed, as if the cop, who was still in the cruiser, could hear her. "You're like way dead. So," she said, drawing the word out, "no driver's license. No car insurance. If they look up your name with the social security office, they'll see you've been dead since the eighteen hundreds!"

"Seventeen hundreds," Alex corrected as he watched the officer step out of his car and approach them. "And stop worrying so much."

"*Seventeen hundreds*?" Lacy squeaked the question in a shrill voice, but never received an answer, because the officer reached Alex's door.

The officer was tall, at least seven feet, and had the large bulk of a weight lifter, but Alex wasn't the least bit intimidated. He'd dealt with far worse than bodybuilding squaddies before. Turning toward the man, he gave what he hoped was an open, repentant expression, and waited.

The officer had a stern expression on his face as he surveyed them. "Do you know why I pulled you over?" he asked, peering at them through light shining from a nearby casino.

Alex answered in a thick Irish brogue, a pleasant smile taking up residence on his face. "Let me start by apologizin', officer. I know I went off the road. My wife got a bat tangled in her hair." He furrowed his brows and shot the officer a look of bafflement. "A bat! We were more than a little surprised by that one. That's why ye were standin' up in yer seat, weren't it, love?"

With a flabbergasted expression, Lacy merely stared at Alex. Finally, after a prompting look from the officer, she slowly nodded her head in confirmation.

Alex slid his gaze back to the officer and offered him a friendly smile as he handed over his driver's license. "She's still a wee bit shaken up about it." He chuckled. "I thought she was goin'ta beat herself to death o'er there."

The officer took the license and proof of insurance Alex provided, his harsh facial expression easing somewhat now that there was a logical explanation for their swerving. "I'll be right back. Sit tight."

As the officer walked off, Lacy spun on Alex. "What was

that?"

He let out a huffy sigh, and without an accent, said, "I'm an Irish immigrant who moved to the States three years ago due to business."

She sucked in a gasp of air. "You gave him a fake ID?"

"It isn't fake. That is my real driver's license, as well as a current insurance card. The date I came over from Ireland is fabricated, but all of my documentation is more or less accurate. I change dates around every few years—"

"You're from Ireland? Like *really* from Ireland?"

"Really," he assured. "I was born in Greece, but my parents crossed the Ionian Sea for work when I was four. Ireland was home to me throughout my mortal life."

"That is so sexy." Her eyes sparkled in delight. "Do the accent again."

Alex rolled his eyes at her and returned his attention to the officer as the man sauntered back over to their car.

"Well, everything checks out," the officer said, handing Alex back his ID and insurance information. His eyes slid to Lacy and he smiled. "I'll let you guys off with a warning this time. Just be careful and try to avoid those pesky bats from here on out."

"Nasty buggers," Alex threw in, his thick accent returning.

Lacy threw in a comment of her own. "I hate those disgusting blood suckers."

The officer nodded his agreement and wandered off.

Alex glanced in her direction as he started up the car. "Most bats don't even drink blood," he corrected. "That's a myth. They usually have a diet of bugs or fruit."

"They usually have a diet of bugs or fruit," Lacy mocked. Leaning forward, she flicked the radio back on. "Geek."

Alex merely frowned at the road in front of him.

"Do you feel a kinship to them? Is that why you feel the need to defend them? Vampire bats. And vampires turn into bats."

"We do not turn into bats," he said with exasperation.

"Hmm." That was her only response. For a few moments, they sat in relative silence, the only sound that of the music, which was thankfully quieter than before. Just as he was getting used to the silence, Lacy turned to look at him with a contemplative expression on her face. "So you've never had oral sex? Ever?"

"Never," Alex said, with only a slight hint of condescension and disgust audible in his voice.

"Hmm." She offered the same response as before. They once again fell into silence. And once again, it was Lacy who made the move for social interaction. "Keep your eyes on the road," she instructed.

"Huh?" Alex glanced at her in confusion as she slid across the bench seat toward him. "What exactly are you doing?" The way she sidled up against him coupled with the mischievous grin she sported had him feeling apprehensive. Since meeting her, he had learned that Lacy was unpredictable, and that smile could mean nothing good.

"Teaching an old dog a new trick."

"Am I the old dog then?" Alex asked in confusion. He forgot all about his question an instant later when Lacy began unzipping the fly of his jeans. "What the hell?" he cried out in surprise.

"Like I said, just keep your eyes on the road," she warned, then lowered her head over his lap.

"Lacy, really..." He wasn't quite sure what game she was playing at, but it wasn't smart to mess with a man while he was driving. As she peeled apart the flap of his boxer shorts, her intentions finally sank in. "Lacy, honestly," he chastised. And then her lips closed over him.

He opened his mouth to demand she sit up properly in her seat, but his breath caught in his throat as she drew her lips slowly up the suddenly hardening length of him, leaving his growing erection wet and chilly in the night air. He swallowed, took a deep breath that he was surprised to find shaky, and tried again. "Lacy—"

He broke off with a gasp as she covered him with her mouth again. Her tongue swirled along the underside of his dick to send chills down his spine. Thirty seconds passed with her licking and sucking before he could find his voice. What he finally said was worlds away from his original objective. "Lacy," he panted. "Don't. Stop." His voice was practically a groan.

She grazed her teeth along him, and he jerked with a hiss. He tried to keep his eyes from crossing, tried to pay attention to the road. His attempt failed when she pulled the entire length of him into her mouth, the head of him sliding down her throat. His foot twitched, pressing down on the gas pedal much harder than he'd intended to.

The car lurched forward, nearly rear-ending the sedan in front of him before Alex found the brake. This led him to the decision that it was safer for their health if he wasn't behind the wheel of the car while she was occupied with his lap. He took the first turn off he found and pulled them into a dark alley. He barely had time to put the car in park before his head fell back against the headrest and he groaned shamelessly.

Lacy gave a soft whimper of desire and doubled her efforts. She added her hand to the mix, wrapping it around the base of him and squeezing.

He thought he might die of pleasure as her hand began stroking him in tandem with the sliding rhythm of her mouth. He'd never done this before, so wasn't quite sure what to do. He wanted to make her aware of his appreciation, though.

Almost shyly, he put his hand on the back of her head and ran his fingers through her silky hair. He tried to concentrate on that simple action to keep himself under control. Still, the sight of her head bobbing up and down as she vigorously sucked at him had him squeezing his eyes tightly closed. Watching her suck his cock was too much, too arousing. His head fell once again to the headrest, and he bit down hard on his lip to keep a growl from escaping.

When her free hand slipped down to caress his testicles, he lost what little control he had. "That's it. You're done." He grabbed her shoulders and pulled her away from his achingly hard cock.

Lacy peered up at him in confusion, blinking her large, innocent eyes. "You didn't like it? I thought for sure you were enjoying yourself. It sounded—" She broke off with a yip as he yanked her toward him.

"I liked it just fine," he said gruffly as he lifted one of her thighs over his lap so she straddled him. "I just need you right here. Right now." Grabbing the back of her head, he kissed her roughly, not caring where her mouth had been moments before. In the same instant, he pulled her down onto his cock.

Lacy gave a gasp of surprise, which quickly turned into a

shuddering moan. "Grimm, I—"

"Don't ruin this," he warned. "Don't say something to embarrass me or throw me off. Let's just do this. I'm begging you."

Lacy pulled back to stare at him. She watched him with contemplative eyes, her warm body sheathing his, before shrugging. "Okay." With that, she wrapped her arms around his neck and drew herself in against his chest. While her body began rocking a seductive dance atop his, she leaned in and nibbled on his earlobe.

Alex hissed, unable to stop himself. "Who's the vampire here?" he asked in breathless amusement. His hands guided her hips, though she needed no assistance in the quick tempo they both silently agreed upon.

This wasn't slow or gentle. This was not at all the type of relationship he'd ever pictured for himself. He was having sex in a car, for crying out loud. This wasn't like him. And that was most of its appeal. He'd never noticed how boring and repetitive his life had become until Lacy forced her way into it.

She was fun. She was zany, and for some unknown reason, she wanted to be with him. In all of his existence, he'd never met anyone like her. It frightened him, but it enthralled him at the same time.

In response to his vampire question, Lacy lowered her mouth over his shoulder and bit down. She bit hard enough to leave a slight indentation of her teeth in his skin, but not hard enough to truly hurt.

Alex gave an unexpected roar of pleasure. It was quite the erotic effect to have someone bite him for a change. Her bite, along with their near frantic rhythm, threw him over the edge. Gripping her hips tightly in his palms, he emptied himself into her welcoming depths.

Her own orgasm seemed to catch her by surprise, because Lacy gave a strangled scream. Her nails dug into his shoulders and she spasmed around him. A moment later, she collapsed tiredly against his chest, her breath escaping in ragged gasps. "I never..." She panted out another exhale. "I never...scream...during sex. You are truly a master. This makes twice you've brought me screaming. You've ruined me for all other men."

"I better have," Alex said gruffly. It wouldn't be so bad if he kept her for his own, right? She was estranged from her family, and she seemed to care about him. In the past, he'd refused to even consider a relationship, especially with a human. It was cruel to them. They had to leave behind their whole lives, their families, because their significant other never aged. He'd seen vampires stick by a mate until they were old and gray. He'd never understood the point of such a thing. It had always seemed unfair.

But Lacy was different. She wouldn't be leaving any family behind. There was no one she would miss. Yet, he had to consider that even though she was enjoying herself now, what would happen when she realized she wanted children? That was something he could never give her. Would she come to resent him for it?

"Stop it," Lacy complained in his ear. "Like you told me, don't ruin it. Stop thinking about what-ifs and coming up with problems. For once, just enjoy yourself."

"How did you..." He trailed off in surprise, his eyes locking on hers.

Lacy ran a finger affectionately along one of his eyebrows. "It's written all over your face. I know you well enough to recognize that expression. You're trying to think of all the reasons why this is a bad idea."

No one besides his sister had ever been close enough to him to be able to know what he was thinking. The fact that Lacy cared enough to pay attention to his mannerisms affected him more than all the amazing sex in the world. Tilting her head back, he kissed her very gently, feeling for the first time in his life what love must be like.

With a grin he wasn't used to wearing, he gave a shrug, mocking her earlier actions. "Okay," he said, repeating her exact same response.

Lacy's lips curved into a soft smile. With a content sigh, she leaned her head against his shoulder, nuzzling his neck with her nose.

"That was so amazing," he whispered into her hair. His lips twitched and a laugh threatened to escape him. "I think I almost defied the laws of physics and turned into a bat."

Lacy snorted, giving an amused chuckle. "You ass."

Chapter Nine

Three days later, Alex stood in the lobby of the hotel next to the racetracks, surveying his surroundings with distaste. Walter hadn't lied to him. The establishment was fully equipped with a ridiculous amount of fake palm trees and chaotic beach adornments. Instead of regular couches in the lobby, there were tacky beach chairs. "I hate this place." He interrupted his sister's in-depth planning to give his opinion of the surrounding décor. "The lounge chairs are terrible."

Regina's eyebrows rose nearly to her hairline. "Okay..." She glanced at the chairs, then back to him. "Are we here to critique the interior decorating or hunt down evil vampires?"

"Ooh! Hunt down evil vampires," Lacy supplied. "Definitely that one."

Alex shot her a dirty look. "That was rhetorical."

"Rhetora-what?" his wife asked shamelessly.

"Focus," Regina advised. "I think we should all concentrate on why we're here. And yes, Lacy, it involves hunting down and killing evil vampires, not making fun of a hotel's theme." With an exaggerated huff and stern eyes for Alex, she continued. "As I was saying...it is nearly impossible to get to the man in charge of the less than legal side of the business. His security is only a minimal few, but they're highly trained. They are taught to sniff out supernatural creatures. If one of us even enters the guy's section, they go on high alert, and he locks himself in some type of panic room he has behind a nearby counter. I guess being in such a shady business, he makes more than his share of enemies. He doesn't play around where security is concerned." She took a deep breath. "Anyway, I had to make my way through two very large and unfriendly bodyguards to get to him. Luckily, they bought my 'Walter's dead' sob story, or I would have been screwed. As it was, I was thoroughly questioned and given a very invasive pat down before I was even allowed near Marcus. That's the man's name, by the way. There is no way you can get close to him without some kind of distraction. And I'm talking a *major* distraction."

Excitement lit Lacy's eyes. "I can be a distraction!"

"Lacy, darling," Alex said gently, his voice full of discouragement. "These people are dangerous."

A stubborn look overtook her features. "I can do this," she stated firmly. "Just give me a chance. I won't be in much danger if I'm only serving as a distraction, right?"

Alex glanced at Regina, who shrugged. "What can it hurt?" she asked. "If she fails, then you'll just have to come at him from another angle." Her expression filled with amusement. "You could always hold me hostage and threaten to kill me if he doesn't talk." Her grin fell only to be replaced with a frown. "Though seeing as I'm his newest, least trusted, and as far as he knows, least trained lackey, he might just tell you to kill me."

"A chance I'm willing to take," Alex teased.

Regina stuck her tongue out in response.

Lacy watched the banter between the two with a crooked grin. "So does this mean I have the green light?"

With reluctance, Alex nodded. "It seems I've been outvoted."

"Looks like," Lacy chirped. Leaning forward, she gave him a quick kiss. As she pulled back, she gave his face a less than gentle love tap with the palm of her hand. "Give me three minutes. I'll provide all the distraction you need." She waved a hand in his direction. "Then you go do your thing. I'll get somewhere safe and call you to come pick me up when it's all over and the bad guys are dead." She took a few steps toward the door that would lead her outside and to the racetracks, then froze. "Um...if I get arrested, please come bail me out. I'm too pretty for prison."

"Arrested?" Alex asked in horror, but Lacy had already skipped out of the hotel. His eyes slid warily to Regina.

She shrugged. "You've already consented. There's no use

trying to change her mind now. Let's go see what sort of theatrics she has cooked up."

As he followed his sister out of the hotel and began the short walk to the racetrack, Alex said, "She had better not do anything dangerous. If I was coerced into allowing my wife to do something in which she gets hurt..." He trailed off at the smirk Regina shot in his direction. "What?"

"Nothing," she lied as they entered the rarely patrolled underside of the metal bleachers. On his glare, Regina's grin widened, and she added, "It's just the *my wife* speech. It's downright adorable. I started out thinking you were slyly trying to find a way out of this marriage, because we all know you refuse to allow yourself even the slightest bit of happiness. I'm second-guessing myself now. I think you might actually love this girl."

Alex frowned in disapproval of her accusations. "My life isn't all misery. I get along just fine with you, and everyone says how fun you are."

Regina rolled her eyes. "You have to get along with me. I'm your sister." She sent him a pointed look. "And *I* am fun. When we go out, *I* dance. *I* drink. *I* hook up with super-hot guys for weekends of bloodletting and sex. *You*, on the other hand," she informed him as they inched closer to the racetrack. "You sit in the corner nursing a juice while frowning at everyone. *You* are decidedly not fun." She shot him an apologetic look at her harsh words. "Sorry." Her expression then became hopeful. "This girl is good for you. She's giving you a personality." As he opened his mouth to protest his lack of a personality, she peered toward the track and spoke over him. "Speaking of your woman...where is she? Her time is about up."

Alex was still frowning at Regina over her tirade about his life. Not only did she call him boring, she didn't even give him the opportunity to attempt to defend himself. He was about to tell her as much when her last comment sank in. He decided to choose responsibility over squabbling with his sibling. "Indeed. Time is up. It looks like we may have to go with your hostage idea."

"Wait," Regina said, putting a hand on his forearm and stopping him just short of the bleacher steps that led up to the section where Marcus conducted his nefarious transactions. "There she is."

He searched the crowd of spectators, looking for Lacy's familiar blonde head. Not finding it, he asked in annoyance, "Where?"

"Not in the stands," Regina said in disbelief. "She's on the track." She shook her head with a chuckle. "She got herself down onto the track!"

Alex's head whipped in the direction Regina spoke of, and there she was. Lacy was moving with purpose toward a lack-luster group of cheerleaders. He couldn't fathom why a race-track had cheerleaders. The crowd didn't care about them, and it was quite apparent they couldn't care less about cheering on the horses either.

Lacy got within a few feet of the women and faltered. Her expression was one of uncertainty, but after a moment, she set her shoulders and marched forward.

When she reached the cheerleaders, Lacy pushed one of the girls roughly to the side, nearly knocking the tall brunette to the grass. "Out of the way, bitches," she said loudly.

A surprised murmur swept through the crowd. It wasn't a complete distraction, but it caught the attention of quite a few people. Of course, Lacy wasn't done yet.

She yanked a megaphone from the hands of one of the other girls. Putting it to her lips, she turned to the crowd and yelled, "Listen up, fuckers!"

Alex cringed as the murmurs grew louder, many people sounding angry at what they'd just been called.

"Are we going to cheer on these fucking horses or what?" Lacy yelled into the megaphone.

There was a mixture of boos, cheers, and some clapping. It didn't matter whether those watching found her offensive or found her funny. Either way, all eyes were suddenly glued to her antics.

"Wow," Regina said with a whistle. "Your woman has some mouth on her."

Alex attempted to frown, but his lips betrayed him by curling into a smirk.

"You're proud of her!" Regina cried with a disbelieving laugh. "Oh my God! You do like her."

He didn't bother answering. Not only because he felt his love life was none of her business, but because he was busy watching Lacy.

She was bouncing around with much more pep than the actual cheerleaders. "Let's make some fucking noise!" she hollered in encouragement. She put the megaphone down and began doing a series of backflips toward the track just as the horses came racing around a turn.

There was a collective gasp of alarm from the spectators as Lacy continued to hurtle herself backwards toward the pounding hooves of the race horses. At the last possible moment, she came to an abrupt stop, her feet inches from the track. With dramatic flair, she raised her hands into the air and threw her head back, looking much like an Olympic gymnast at the end of a routine.

He sucked in a breath of relief as the crowd burst into raucous cheers.

Regina let out a little chuckle. "Guess her plan worked." She nodded toward the section their vampire haunted. "She's got everyone watching her every move. Including you."

Alex glanced up into the bleachers and saw that Regina was correct. Every eye in the building was glued to Lacy. Right now, they wouldn't notice a bus plowing through. Every last person in the stands, the vampire guards included, were holding their collective breaths to see what the blonde vixen would do next.

"Let's get moving," Alex instructed, lowering his voice with grim determination.

Regina put a hand to his forearm, halting his progress. "I can't go with you. At least not at your side. They think I'm one of them. I have to hang back for a few minutes. I'm supposed to be patrolling the perimeter of the building, and I don't want to risk blowing my cover." She took a step away from him and added, "Leave a few of them alive, so me surviving doesn't seem suspicious. I'll see you in a few days when you take the asshole running this operation down. Further contact between us until then is probably unwise."

Alex nodded. He understood completely. Regina and Lacy had done everything for him they could. Now it was his turn to deliver results. Squaring his shoulders, he stepped out from under the cover of the bleachers and began marching up the steps to the section Marcus occupied. It was nearly empty, the occupants consisting only of Marcus and a few other vampires. They'd obviously done their best to keep the man unreachable, but Lacy was a good enough distraction that they didn't see him coming.

The vampire had his eyes locked onto whatever antics Lacy was currently up to. In fact, every single lackey nearby was doing the same exact thing. Every one of the vampire's guards were neglecting their jobs. They were too busy watching the diversion on the track to realize something was off. Alex was amazed at how easy it was to get to his target.

As he marched up the bleachers, Alex heard the crowd gasp and fought the urge to turn around and make sure Lacy was okay. He trusted her not to get herself seriously injured. Instead, he closed the distance of the last few feet separating him and Marcus. He grabbed the other man by the collar and yanked him to his feet. "I'd say it's about time you and I had a talk, Marcus. Come this way."

Drawing on his supernatural strength, Alex was able to drag Marcus up the few remaining steps to the ticket booth before the other man could realize what was happening and call for help.

He locked the door behind them, but knew it would do little to keep out a group of pissed off vampires once they realized what was going on. Throwing Marcus against the wall, he held the vampire there with one hand and jammed a chair underneath the doorknob with his other. As soon as that task was done, he returned his attention to his unwilling company. "I think you know what I'm here for."

Marcus gulped and squirmed in Alex's grip. "I...I know."

Alex squeezed down on the man's windpipe as pounding sounded at the door. "You know what I did to Walter. I would think it best for you all around if you just tell me what I want to know. It will be less painful that way." He loosened his grip slightly, giving the other vampire room to speak.

He had barely shifted his fingers before Marcus started spewing words in a hurried, breathless voice. "The man you seek operates out of the Caribbean Chateau. It's not on the main drag. It's out of the way, on the borderline of being obsolete. It's easier for him to keep a low profile this way." He swallowed thickly before adding, "The man you're looking for goes by the name of Shapiro Langston."

Alex blinked in surprise as the information came rolling

off the vampire's tongue. He pulled Marcus away from the wall a few inches before shoving him roughly back against it. "That was way too easy," he growled.

His eyes narrowing in anger, Marcus spat out his response. "I'm not dying for that prick. With him gone, I move up the food chain. I figure either my men kill you in about thirty seconds or you prove yourself resourceful enough to get to Shapiro and take him out of the game. Either way, I win."

"You're assuming I'm not going to kill you."

"Kill me?" Marcus asked in disbelief. "Why would you kill me? I've been one hundred percent cooperative. The worst I did was have my way with a few of the girls, drank a little blood, which is minor in the scheme of things. I could be a good contact for you. Killing me would only hurt you in the end." He grinned haughtily, his expression becoming nearly condescending. "I know how you bleeding hearts hate to take lives. You don't kill cooperative witnesses. It goes against everything you stand for."

Alex nodded thoughtfully to this reasoning. He then gave a cruel smile as he yanked a stake from his duster pocket. Leaning in, he put his face even with Marcus's. "I'm not as good as you think." With that, he slammed the stake forward into the vampire's chest.

Marcus's eyes widened a second before the wood punctured his heart. He didn't have time to scream or beg for mercy before his body disintegrated into dust.

Feeling one step close to his end goal, Alex pocketed the stake and turned toward the door, preparing to fight his way through an angry mob of vampires. They were going to be even more pissed when they realized their boss was nothing more than ash.

With a weary sigh at the knowledge that he was about to come away from this at the very least with a black eye, Alex removed the chair.

Someone pounded on the other side of the door, and wood near the hinges groaned in protest as little slivers broke away under the force.

"What the hell?" Alex asked aloud. "Why not add property damage to my list of crimes today?" With that, he lifted his foot and kicked the door the rest of the way off the hinges.

Even though they were trained for aggression, the six vampires jumped in surprise at having their intended target come out to meet them head on. They were obviously used to someone more submissive, which Alex wouldn't hesitate to use to his advantage. He whipped his recovered stake in the closest vampire's direction. It lodged into the man's chest, but didn't sink deep enough to reach the heart. With a sigh, Alex paused, lined up a kick, and drove the stake home with his booted foot.

The vampire dropped to his knees with a howl. He only had a moment to paw at his chest before he crumbled into ash. This left the bodyguard count at five, not including Regina.

Just as he was thinking of his sister, she popped up in front of him with a feral hiss. He cringed and took a surprised step back. It wasn't often he found himself on the receiving end of her "game face." That was usually reserved for the times he did something incredibly stupid—like accidentally knocking her into a swimming pool at a party full of eligible male vampires. In his defense, he was socially awkward. He'd been born that way and there didn't seem to be any cure for it. She'd tried.

Snapping out of his reverie, Alex returned her snarl, and with a silent plea for forgiveness, he hit Regina with a right hook to the eye.

She went down, flying over a few seats to land on the floor. She wasn't dead, which meant she'd heal. He'd have to be satisfied with that.

Having no other choice, Alex turned his back on her and faced the remaining five men. One of them was directly in his path. Reacting by instinct, Alex grabbed the vampire by the shoulders and threw him forcefully down the stairs.

The vampire rolled down the bleachers, each bounce against the metallic steps sounding painful. There was a dull *bong* as the man connected with the railing at the bottom of the seating section and went still.

"Where is Marcus?" a voice snarled in his ear a moment before Alex took a shot to the kidneys. He groaned and almost dropped to his knees. He only managed to stay on his feet because he knew if he went down, he would more than likely never get back up. Pushing the pain to the back of his mind, he spun to face the vampire who'd punched him. Whipping another stake from the deep pockets of his jacket, he jammed it into the vampire's chest in one smooth motion as he completed the turn. "So much for highly trained," he said to the ashes as they fell to clump on the edges of his boots.

Out of the corner of his eye, he saw the remaining three vampires moving in his direction, and Regina was getting to her feet. Luckily, the vampire who'd taken the headlong dive down the steps still wasn't moving; he appeared to be unconscious.

"I'm outta here," Alex informed them a moment before he lunged over a nearby handrail, dropping to the seating section below. He hit the cement, gave his knees a moment to absorb the impact, and then he was running.

He bolted out of the stands, out of the open building. He was to the parking lot and peeling out before any of the confused and disorganized vampires even reached the next level of bleachers. Regina would have to fend for herself the next couple of days.

He knew she'd kick his ass for worrying about it, but she was his sister. He couldn't help himself. He hated the thought of leaving her alone in the hands of men who didn't think twice about committing murder.

Still, she was good at this, and despite his concern, he had every confidence in her abilities. He needed to let her do her job. All that was left for him was to wait for Lacy's call to tell him where to pick her up.

Chapter Ten

Lacy's requested pick up call came in the form of her one phone call from jail. Alex spent the following hour apologizing to the local police department for his wife's outlandish behavior and listening to their disbelief over her negative breathalyzer results. They'd discovered she wasn't drunk, but possibly mentally unbalanced. They suggested a trip to a psychologist.

After assuring that he'd seek professional help, Alex was ushered to the back to see Lacy. She was seated on a long bench between a large woman with a mullet and a very stoned-looking woman whose midlife crisis was made apparent by her bleached blonde hair, Miley Cyrus t-shirt, and jelly-band bracelets.

As soon as she saw him, Lacy jumped up from her seat with a smile and raced to the bars.

Alex watched her make her way over in total admiration. It was hard not to appreciate her looks. He started at her feet, taking in her knee-high black boots. His eyes roved hungrily over the bare expanse of her legs until he came to the lilac-colored shorts that were so tiny they were barely worth mentioning. His gaze swept up to her fitted black t-shirt, lingering an extra second on her perky breasts before continuing up to her eyes.

He couldn't help but smile in return as they made eye contact. Only Lacy could pull off purple Daisy-Dukes and knee-high boots. "You were right," he admitted fondly. "You *are* too pretty for prison."

Lacy tilted her head to the side, her smirk becoming teasing. "Does this mean you've come to bail me out and take me home with you?"

He knew his eyes had to be darkening with lust at the suggestion in her voice. "Yeah," he said gruffly. "I've come to take you home."

Rolling his eyes, the guard behind Alex unlocked the cell door. It opened with a loud, metallic squeak. "He's signed all the necessary paperwork. You're a lucky woman. If it was me, I'd have let you sit in here for the night to think about your actions."

Alex suspected the guard's significant other didn't look nearly as fabulous in shorts as Lacy...or as good out of them.

As the guard stepped back to allow her through, Lacy rushed forward and leapt into Alex's arms. Her legs wrapped around his waist and her arms circled his neck. "I was so worried." Her words were a breathy whisper against his jaw.

Alex smiled. Holding her with one arm braced under her bottom, he patted the guard on the shoulder with his free hand. "Like I said, too pretty for prison." Not letting Lacy go, he walked out of the precinct and into the balmy Nevada night. "Now what were you so worried about?" he asked playfully, responding when she gave him a firm kiss.

When she finally pulled back from their kiss, Lacy's eyes were full of concern. "The cheerleaders were vampires."

"What?" The comment was so unexpected, he wasn't sure he'd heard her correctly.

"The cheerleaders were vampires," she repeated.

His heart plummeting, he lowered her to the pavement. She'd been in mortal danger simply by acting as a distraction. He wouldn't have thought...

"I was so worried about you because the cheerleaders were vampires." Before he could ask how that worried her for him, she continued. "You went in thinking there were half a dozen vampires when there were potentially many more. If the cheerleaders were vampires, who knew how many more they had crawling about that place."

Alex took her face in his hands, his eyes widening in horror as understanding dawned on him. "That's why you hesitated. You realized what they were."

"Yeah, it threw me for a moment," she admitted.

"But you went ahead with your plan anyway?" His words were full of disbelief. If she'd been aware of the risk, he couldn't fathom why she would have continued with her task.

Lacy blinked at him as if confused by his question. "Of course I did." She reached her hand up to cover his. "I knew it was important to your case."

"Lacy, you could have been hurt!" His eyes desperately searched her face for understanding. He wanted to make sure she realized he didn't want her in any danger. "Your safety is more important than this case."

Her eyes widened, her expression becoming one of shock. "Alex," she said, using his first name for the first time he could recollect, "I love you." Wrapping her arms around his waist, she stepped forward. Standing on her tiptoes, she kissed his chin. Smiling affectionately up at him, she said, "It melts my heart that you are concerned for my welfare. I wasn't in any real danger, though. I know I pissed off those eternally skanky bitches, but there wasn't much they could do. I had every eye in the stands on me. No matter how annoying I got, they couldn't rip my throat open and drain me. It would have drawn too much attention. You were the one in danger, not me. If any of those nasty vampires would have hurt you..." She rubbed her cheek against his palm.

"I can handle myself just fine," he assured. It was odd having someone worried about him. Being a private detective, he was used to doing the worrying. Even his own sister didn't worry about him. She'd lived so long that she seemed to think they were invincible, a trait that often worried him.

Lacy lowered her hands to his chest, placing her palm over his heart. "I know you can handle yourself. It's still my job to worry about you, though." She tilted her head to the side with a small smile as she studied his face. "I know us being married is a product of way too much alcohol, but I take the vows we exchanged seriously. It may have only been in front of a couple of Elvis impersonators, but I did promise to take care of you."

At the mention of their irrational, impromptu wedding, Alex took a deep breath. "Speaking of nuptials..." He wasn't sure if he was going to ask her for an annulment or beg her never to leave him. His emotions were a constant war within him. He wanted her, yet he wanted to remove her from the danger that was his life.

He didn't get to find out what the rest of his sentence

would be, because she gasped loudly and interrupted him. "Oh no! Bianca and Bernard's wedding!"

He jumped in surprise at her sudden outburst. "What?"

"Bernard and Bianca! Their wedding is..." She looked at her wrist, realized she wasn't wearing a watch, and then snatched his wrist to turn his watch to face her. "It's like fourteen hours away!" Grabbing his arm, she pulled him frantically toward the parking lot.

Alex followed after her, confused by her urgency. "There's still an hour before sun up. They aren't getting married until this evening. You have plenty of time..." He trailed off when Lacy spun on him with wild eyes.

"Plenty of time?" she screeched. "I have *no* time. Because of your vampire schedule, I've been sleeping during the day. Ten hours of beauty sleep is the absolute minimum when a wedding is involved."

She located his car and shoved him impatiently toward the driver's side before simply hopping over the door on her side of the convertible. "That leaves me four hours from right now. And that doesn't even include time to get ready." She gave a squeak of horror. "We don't even have a gift yet."

Alex slid into the driver's seat and started up the car. Calmly turning to look at her, he said, "The man cheated on you with your best friend. And don't even get me started on Bianca. Fuck them. They don't deserve a gift."

Lacy blinked big blue eyes at him for a moment. "Not give them a gift." She sat in silence as if she was trying to get a feel for that statement. Spinning in her seat, she turned her body to face his. "Can we do that? Is it allowed?"

Alex shot her a grin. "Like I said earlier, fuck 'em." He waved a hand in her direction as they started the short drive back to their hotel. "What dilemma can I help you with next?" he inquired, feeling pleased with his problem solving skills.

"Well..." She bit her lip and eyed him hesitantly.

"Don't be shy," he encouraged. "Lay it on me."

Lacy paused only a moment longer before taking a deep breath. "I'm not insulting your wardrobe, but I haven't seen you wear anything fancy enough for a wedding. We need to buy you a suit."

"Not necessary," Alex said with a wink in her direction. "I

keep a suit in the trunk of my car for emergencies. As a private detective, I never know when I might need something."

She stared at him in apparent amazement. "Okay...that really helps."

Deciding the bubble of energy he'd somehow attached himself to needed a little teasing to lighten her mood, he said, "Though I never agreed to go to this wedding. If you want me to be your date, I think you should probably ask me out."

Her jaw dropped in disbelief. "You..." Narrowing her eyes, Lacy crossed her arms over her chest. "We're married. I don't have to ask. It should be assumed."

His lips twitched in amusement at her outrage. "Well, the proper course of a relationship would be to date, get to know one another, in today's day and age. Next would be sexual intimacy, and finally, marriage. We are doing things ass backwards. I'm still fuzzy on the details. I believe we got married first...after what, an hour?"

Realizing he was only teasing her, Lacy grinned. "Yeah. Couldn't have been much more than that before you confessed you couldn't live without me. Drunken dummy," she said affectionately.

"Very dumb," he agreed. "Seeing as how I'm not even alive." He ignored the tongue she stuck out at him. "So let's see... Next on our reversed list is sex. I believe we covered that more than satisfactorily. From what you've told me, we took care of that right away. There was the elevator, the hotel swimming pool, our hotel room... Am I missing anywhere?"

"The hotel roof," she said with a giggle.

Alex was glad they were at a red light, because his head whipped automatically in her direction. "*What*?"

"You wanted our first time together to be romantic and special. You took me up to the roof so we could make love under the stars. You said you wanted to see my naked skin shine in the moonlight while I moved on top of you."

"Dear God," he wheezed at that mental image, his grip tightening on the steering wheel until his knuckles turned white.

"Very romantic."

"Romantic...yes. That's what I was thinking." As the light turned to green, he inched forward and made a quick left into their parking lot. "Like I said, we totally had that requirement filled. Next on the list would be getting to know each other. I feel we've been doing that quite well these past few days. I've learned you are reckless. You're unpredictable and possibly insane. Also, you have a violent temper. Bernard's car looked like it had suffered a werewolf attack after you were done with that tire iron." The dirty look he received in response made him smile.

"Let me have a turn at this." Lacy requested this with a wave of her hand. "Let's see... You're unbearably stubborn. You have to be in control of even the tiniest aspect of your life. You plan everything to death. And for a vampire, you're very stuffy."

"On the flipside..." He pulled into a parking space, not at all insulted by her on-the-mark observations. "You have the sweetest blood I've ever tasted, and your energy is intoxicating."

"You have the biggest cock I've ever seen," Lacy complimented as she climbed out of the car. "And despite your best efforts, you actually come off as quite romantic at times."

Alex joined her at the front of the car as they trekked toward their hotel. "All in all, this is somehow working out. We're exact opposites. I think we keep each other—"

"Balanced." They both spoke the word simultaneously.

Lacy turned to look at him with a small smile. Alex eyed her from head to toe, taking in her beautiful features. He still couldn't fathom how a woman like her could wish to attach herself to him.

She reached out to touch her hand against his with a light, affectionate brush. The gesture lasted but a moment before she turned and marched purposefully into the hotel. She shoved through the lobby and into the elevators, returning to wedding mode. "Now," she said briskly. "Back to my dilemma. You may have a suit, but I don't have a hair stylist. Bridesmaids are supposed to have their hair done by a professional. I'd planned on making an appointment shortly after getting into town, but then I met you and things got a little crazy." She took a deep breath and let it out with a huff. "By this point, it's going to be impossible to get in with even a mediocre stylist. I'm screwed. I'm going to look totally frumpy."

"Lace, there isn't a frumpy thing about you." He followed her into the elevator and pressed the button for their floor.

"And you don't have to worry about a hair stylist. I've got it covered."

"No offense," she said slowly and with a frown, "but I don't think now is the best time for you to try to learn how to use a curling iron. I don't want to be showing up with burn marks on my neck."

"Oh hell no! *I'm* not doing your hair." He shuddered at the thought. "As soon as I heard about the wedding, an idea began churning in my head. After I killed Walter, I called Gabriel to inform him of how much he owes us. I hinted that he could repay us by sending the best stylist he's got over to the hotel room on the day of the wedding to get you girlied up. Of course, he insisted that was himself. He said to allot him three hours to give you the works. He said something about a pedicure, a facial, hair, makeup, you name it. He's giving you the full-on, personal treatment."

"You are the greatest man in the world," Lacy proclaimed, throwing her arms around his neck.

Alex laughed and wrapped an arm around her waist. His palm touched bare flesh where her shirt had risen up, causing heat to sizzle through him. "Glad I could help." His thumb caressed the skin of her back, and his hips moved forward to nestle against hers.

His sudden rush of attraction to her caught him off guard. He knew he shouldn't be surprised. Everything she did seemed to arouse him. She could be vacuuming, and he'd still find it sexy, still have to fight the uncontrollable urge to have sex with her. He couldn't restrain himself. She was irresistible.

She must have sensed where his thoughts were going, because her irises darkened with lust. "I know we've already had sex there, but would you be terribly against repeating our shower extravaganza? I want to get this broad chest wet and rub myself all over it."

Alex groaned. He lowered his mouth to hers and walked her backwards out of the elevator toward their door. "You're trying to kill me," he said with a growl into her mouth.

"You're already dead."

Alex let go of her long enough to get the door open and usher her inside.

She was barely out of view of the hallway before she pulled her shirt over her head. "Am I to take that bulge in your pants as an acceptance of my shower proposal?"

"Damn right you are," he said, voice low and full of arousal. "I figure with your ten hours of beauty sleep and Gabriel's beautification time, we still have a good forty minutes."

Lacy stepped out of her shorts, leaving herself in a thong, her bra, and the massive boots. "For multiple orgasms, I'm willing to lose a few hours of sleep. That's got to be more relaxing anyway."

Alex snatched up the "Do Not Disturb" sign and shoved it on the outer doorknob. "Trust me, I plan on making any sleep you lose thoroughly worth it."

***

Alex awoke to the sound of pounding on the door of his hotel room. With an annoyed groan, he rolled out of bed. Still half asleep, he picked up an old-fashioned looking gun from the bedside stand. The gun only looked old-fashioned; it was actually quite new. It was a unique piece, as it fired wooden bullets. It was a favorite in his collection, but he only used it in extreme cases...like being sleep-deprived due to a very bendy ex-cheerleader.

The gun made for a quicker kill, but bullets were hard to come by. Besides, the less he used the gun, the less likely it was anyone would find out about its existence. It was nice to have the element of surprise if a fight started to turn south, though that was something that hadn't happened to him in a long time.

He mostly kept the gun as a type of security blanket. He'd only actually ever used it twice. Once when a rabid vampire had been chowing down on a four year old girl. And once to save his sister's life. Any other time, he preferred a good, old-fashioned stake...except now. Now he was too exhausted to care.

Barely opening his eyes, he trudged to the door and looked through the peephole. "What?" He grumbled this to the person in the hallway. When his bleary eyes focused, he said, "Oh. It's you. Hold on." He spun to Lacy, who was just sitting up in bed with a tired yawn. "It's the hair guy," he explained as he opened the door.

"The hair guy?" Gabriel asked with offense as he bustled into the room carrying two large bags in his hands. "I have a name, you know. It's Gabriel Valenchino Allenzo Caprichio." He winked. "But you can just call me Gabe." That being said, his eyes slid to Lacy and he gave a horrified gasp. "Dear lord!"

Lacy's gaze shot down to her fully exposed breasts. With a cry of alarm, she yanked the comforter up to cover herself. "You could have given me a minute to get decent."

Gabriel gave a derisive snort. "Darling, please. Like I want to see your boobies." He glanced at Alex over his shoulder. "Now *him* I will guiltily admit to ogling." His eyes narrowed at him. "Your legs are very distracting. If you want me to get any work done, I suggest you throw on some pants." He fanned his face as his eyes traveled up the entire length of Alex's body. "Damn. It's suddenly getting very hot in here."

Alex glanced down at himself to realize he was in nothing more than his boxer shorts. He quickly snatched his pants up from the floor and scrambled into them. He'd never had to worry about such things before this week. Gay vampires. It was...preposterous.

"Thank you," Gabriel said with a cheeky grin before turning his attention back to Lacy. He shared a conspiratorial smirk with her. "He has the nicest nipples."

Lacy nodded with a girly giggle. "I know. I can't keep myself from nibbling them."

With a frown, Alex crossed his arms over his chest, covering the topic of discussion.

Gabriel gave a deep, throaty laugh and sat on the edge of the bed next to Lacy. "Now, onto the reason for my horrified gasp." He reached out and gingerly touched her mussed hair. "Honey, did a raccoon die in here?"

Lacy's eyes lifted skyward as she tried to eye her own hair. "That bad, huh?"

Gabriel snorted. Opening one of his bags, he riffled around and pulled out a can. Shaking it, he sprayed a clear liquid into his palm, then lathered it into Lacy's hair. "That should take some of the frizz out." He swept a hand dramatically toward the bathroom. "Now please go brush your teeth. I can't work under these conditions."

Lacy scrambled to her feet and scurried off to the bathroom, trailing the sheet behind her. "I'll be right back," she called over her shoulder.

Alex watched her disappear in amazement. "How did you do that?" he asked Gabriel in awe. "No argument. No dragging her feet. She just got up and did what you asked without a fuss. Unbelievable."

Gabriel shrugged. "She knows when I speak to her, I'm not thinking with my dick. You are. I am merely looking out for her welfare."

Alex made a choking sound in his throat. "Excuse me? I do not—"

Gabriel cut him off. "When I showed up here, she was naked in your bed. You answered the door with not much more on. She'd obviously engaged in sexual relations with you recently." His eyes swept over Alex's chest. "Lucky girl."

Not even attempting to go for casual, Alex snatched his shirt up from the floor and pulled it over his head. To the accusation of him thinking with his dick, he said, "I'm not that type of guy."

At that moment, Lacy moseyed out of the bathroom. She'd climbed into undergarments, but Alex still found it hard not to gawk at her in appreciation. His eyes followed the subtle bounce of her breasts and the juicy curves of her backside as she sauntered past him.

"You *are* that type of guy." Gabriel clicked his tongue with disapproval before turning to Lacy. "Come here, sweetie. Let's get you into some clothes before the wolf gets you."

Alex wasn't particularly pleased with being referred to as a wolf, but he supposed he deserved it. Though it was against his usual character, he found he couldn't keep his thoughts from turning sexual where Lacy was concerned. With a grunt at his own lack of self-control, he said, "I'll get out of your way. Just let me know when I'm needed." With that, he grabbed a book and settled himself on the bed.

Over the next few hours, Alex did his best to tune out the giggles and outpouring of gossip that swirled about the room. Having a gay man in his hotel room was bad enough, but a gay vampire was a tragedy. There was no way Lacy was walking away from this encounter full of the fear and awe his kind deserved. Instead, she was going to think they were all teddy bears.

At another bout of uncontrollable laughter, Alex rolled his

eyes. "Are the two of you almost finished?" he asked, trying to keep the impatience in his voice down to a minimum.

Apparently, he failed, because Gabriel made a sound of disgust. "A straight man and a vampire. How do you stand it?" he asked Lacy.

"He's really good in bed," she said flippantly in reply.

Alex lowered his book in outrage. "Is that all I am to you? A good lay?" When his eyes landed on Lacy, he froze. She looked...amazing.

"We're done," Gabriel said with dramatic flair. "What do you think?"

Alex surveyed his wife from head to toe. Lacy's hair was swept up in dozens of spiral curls. A few were left loose, resting tantalizingly against her neck. There was some type of glitter gel lathered into her hair, causing it to catch in the light and sparkle.

His gaze then moved to her face. Her makeup had been tastefully done. Pretty, sea green eye shadow brought out the color of her eyes while the pale pink lipstick had him itching to kiss her full, sensual lips. There was more glitter along her throat and collarbone.

Unable to help himself, Alex slid to his feet and crossed the room to her. He reached a hand out to caress that sparkling exposed flesh just above her breasts. His eyes lowered to admire the cleavage that threatened to escape the square neckline of her sea green bridesmaid dress. His index finger followed the path of his eyes, brushing against the swell of her breasts.

His gaze followed the lines of the dress, noting the way it hugged her every curve, making her hips look more sexual than any dress should allow. When he finished admiring everything down to her adorable toes, he lifted his gaze back to hers. "Wow. You are the most gorgeous bridesmaid ever to exist."

"I was an even better looking bride," she said softly, a grin touching her lips.

Alex slid his hand up from her neck to the back of her head, cradling it gently in his palm. "I wish I could remember." He lowered his mouth to hers, caressing ever so gently along her bottom lip.

Lacy gave a soft sound of pleasure and her eyelashes

fluttered closed.

Alex slid his palm along her hip, giving a low groan at the feel of silk and skin beneath his hand.

Gabriel was suddenly grabbing Alex's shoulder, pushing him back. "Down, boy."

Alex whirled on him with a snarl, his fangs protruding menacingly. His grip tightened possessively on Lacy's hip as he stared the other man down.

"Grimm!" Lacy slapped his chest, reminding him that his behavior was not socially acceptable, especially when it was directed at someone who had just helped them out.

Where most sane men would, Gabriel didn't back down from the fangs. "I will not have that attitude, mister! I spent way too much time making her beautiful for you to muss her up with your big gorilla hands."

Frowning, Alex tucked his hands under his armpits. He'd never considered himself one of those macho, caveman types. Being treated like one wasn't something he enjoyed.

"Besides..." Gabriel continued on as if he wasn't the least bit worried Alex would harm him. "You need to get yourself dressed. We're finished here."

Alex nodded meekly and moved toward his suitcase. Before he made it there, he froze in astonishment as Gabriel reached down to the hem at the feet of Lacy's dress and gave it a vicious yank at the seam. The fabric tore, leaving a slit that traveled all the way up Lacy's calf, ending scandalously high up on her thigh. Her body jerked with the violent tug, her breasts straining against the tight fabric.

Alex blinked in surprise. He wasn't sure whether to be offended or extremely turned on.

"Gabe!" Lacy said in disbelief.

The stylist backed away from her, dusting his hands off against each other. "There. Now we're ready." He leaned forward and brushed a piece of lint off Lacy's shoulder. "That was *just* what this dress needed. If anyone questions you, just say the hem split when you were climbing out of the car. It's so damn tight, no one will doubt you."

She stared at him for a moment, her blue eyes wide with the shock of having her dress shredded as if it was no firmer than a scrap of paper. She gingerly touched one of the curls at her neck, her movements almost nervous. "Okay..." After another brief silence, she said, "I guess there's only one thing left to do."

"Besides the oaf getting dressed," Gabriel said with a pointed look at Alex.

Alex frowned in response. He didn't know what was worse, Gabriel hitting on him or Gabriel bitching at him.

Ignoring Gabriel, Lacy took a deep breath and turned to face her husband. "Grimm..." She took one of his hands in hers and gazed angelically up at him. "Will you be my date to the wedding?"

Alex gave an unexpected bark of laughter at her request. Their earlier conversation of how ass-backwards their relationship had progressed filled his mind, and he rewarded her with an affectionate smile. Leaning down, he kissed her, being careful not to smudge her makeup. "Baby, for you, I'd murder the pope."

Chapter Eleven

Alex sat in the fifth row of the church where Bianca and Bernard were to be married. The bride had just made her way down the aisle, and everyone was gushing about how beautiful she was. His eyes were all for Lacy, though.

She looked like an angel up there at the altar. He couldn't keep himself from imagining her in a flowing white gown, her cheeks flushed pink with delight. He could almost picture himself standing next to her, a groom to her bride. He made a sound of discomfort and shifted in his seat. He wasn't a romantic, nor was he usually prone to such thoughts.

He turned his musings instead to the humor of the concern Lacy had shown upon their arrival at the church. He'd had to calm her down and assure her that he could in fact enter a church without bursting into flames. Vampirism was a virus, not a sign of Satanism. There were bad vampires, just as there were bad humans in the world. The majority of the supernatural community were upstanding citizens. Like him.

He was so preoccupied with these thoughts and Lacy's appearance that he didn't notice the vampire creeping toward the altar until it was too late. Alex saw the man an instant before he grabbed the bride and yanked her in front of him.

"Alex!" The vampire yelled the word, his voice echoing through the church. "Alex Grimm! My boss would like a word with you."

Alex was on his feet in a heartbeat. He didn't even stop to think about slinking down in his seat or hiding. He wouldn't let anyone be harmed if this man was looking for him.

His gaze shot to Lacy. Her eyes were wide and frightened

as she took a step backwards away from the scuffle. As she backed up, she bumped into the chest of a second vampire.

"I don't think so." The vampire growled loud enough to make a few attendees gasp in fear as they realized something was terribly wrong. "No one's going anywhere until we get Alex Grimm."

Alex stepped out into the aisle, relief filling him that he'd chosen an aisle seat. Climbing over frightened humans while trying to keep his eyes on the vampires might have been tricky. "Let them go. I'm the one you want."

"Damn right you're the one we want." The vampire holding Bianca shook her rough enough to cause some of her hair to come loose of its up-do. "You've been causing Mr. Langston trouble for some time now, but taking out our contact at the racetrack was his last straw."

Alex fought to keep the surprise from showing on his face. He'd only recently discovered who Shapiro Langston was. Apparently, the other man had known of *him* for longer. So much for being discreet in his line of work...

Trying not to set the vampire off, Alex inched forward slowly. He struggled to keep his gaze from returning to Lacy. These men knew more about him already than he'd realized, but if there was a chance they didn't know he and Lacy were together, it would be safer for her. "Just let the bride go, and we can talk."

The man's hand flew to Bianca's throat, clenching down on her windpipe. "Take one step closer and she's dead," he warned.

Bianca made a strangled sound in the back of her throat. Tears sprang to her eyes from the force being used against her neck. She struggled feebly for a moment until the vampire gave a vicious jerk. She emitted a whimper of pain, then went still in his grip, the fight leaving her.

Alex froze in his tracks. He didn't doubt for a moment that this man would kill her. They did business by murdering those who didn't pay their debts; they wouldn't think twice about killing someone with no financial ties to their boss. She was nothing more than a piece in their sadistic game, one they were willing to sacrifice.

Alex didn't like Bianca, but he didn't want to see her dead either. "I'm not moving," he assured. "I'll do whatever you want. Just leave these people alone. They have nothing to do with this."

"Does it bother you? Us killing innocent humans?" The vampire grinned wickedly. "Maybe I should snap her neck just to teach you a lesson. You're at this wedding. You must know these people. Killing the bride would certainly send home the message that you don't *fuck* with Shapiro's business!"

Alex remained perfectly still as he tried to assess the situation. Any movement on his part would result in the forfeit of innocent lives. He knew that well and certain. He needed to handle this situation very prudently.

Out of the corner of his eye, he saw Lacy inching toward Bianca and the vampire. To anyone else, it would appear as if she was trying to edge away from the vampire behind her, but he recognized the purposeful glint in her eyes. He silently tried to convey to her not to do anything dangerous.

She ignored him, moving closer still to the hostage situation. When she was a few feet away, Lacy charged at the vampire. She hit him with her shoulder, knocking him forward.

He released his grip on Bianca, who tumbled to her hands and knees on the floor.

While the vampire stood stunned by the unexpected attack, Lacy pulled her leg back and kicked him in the groin from behind. When he dropped, she jumped onto his back, pressing one of her knees into his spine. "Grimm," she hollered out. "Help!"

His heart in his throat, Alex raced forward, yanking a pair of handcuffs from his back pocket. He kept them for situations such as this, where he couldn't use lethal force. Staking a vampire in a church full of humans would not be good.

As he reached Lacy, he nudged her out of the way and grabbed the vampire's wrists, slapping the cuffs on. "Are you out of your mind?" he growled at his wife.

She shrugged nonchalantly. "It worked, didn't it?" Glancing down, she fingered the slit in her dress. "Gabriel was right. This *was* necessary. I never would have been able to climb onto his back without being able to move my legs. The original design was too restrictive."

Alex looked at her with disbelief, though he didn't get to comment because something behind her caught his attention.

The second vampire seemed to snap out of his stunned

stupor at Lacy's unexpected attack. He grabbed her by the upper arms and spun her around to face him.

Reacting on instinct, Lacy curled her hand into a fist and punched him in the mouth.

The vampire reeled back, stunned. It took him only a moment to regain himself. He shoved Lacy roughly, knocking her to her backside. Straightening himself to his full height, he swept his eyes to his restrained companion. Those eyes then slipped to Alex. The maliciousness in their depths fizzled out as he seemed to realize he was no longer in control of the situation.

When Alex moved forward menacingly, the vampire shot one last look at his comrade before he turned and ran. He raced to the doorway behind the pulpit and disappeared from sight.

Alex considered giving chase, but quickly dismissed the idea. Instead, he addressed the anxious crowd. "I'm a police officer," he lied. "Please stay calm."

"Stay calm?" Bianca asked in a shrill voice as she slowly picked herself up off the ground. A cough wracked her body, and she rubbed at her reddened throat. "*Stay calm*?"

Alex eyed her appearance with a cringe. Where her groom was unruffled and nearly disinterested in things going on around him, Bianca's hair was in tangles and mascara streaked across her cheeks in thick, ugly black lines. On the front of her gown was a large, unidentifiable stain.

Spinning on Lacy, she pointed an accusing finger. "You've ruined my wedding!" Her face turned red with rage. "You brought your stupid detective in here, and druggies followed you! You're a horrible best friend! This is supposed to be the happiest day of my life, and you destroyed it!"

Alex saw the expression on Lacy's face and winced. This was going to be ugly.

"Ruined *your* wedding?" Lacy hollered as she squared her feet as if preparing for an argument. "*Are you kidding me*? You stole *my* wedding. You stole my fiancé! If anyone's a terrible friend, it's you!"

Bianca took a step back and blinked in surprise. "Excuse me?"

Lacy took an intimidating step forward and poked Bianca in the chest. "What you did to me was unforgivable. We're not cool, and quite frankly, I think you're a shitty friend." She spun wrathfully to face Bernard. "And *you*! All men do *not* cheat. That is bullshit, you scumbag." On a roll, she spun to face a man in the front row. "While we're on the subject of scumbags, it is *not* acceptable to grope your son's girlfriend, you old pervert! You need to learn to keep your hands to yourself!"

The man's cheeks flushed bright red, and he slunk down into his seat as if trying to disappear from all the eyes that were suddenly turned in his direction.

With a huff at the man's cowardice, Lacy spun to Alex. "Let's take the prisoner and get out of here." She whirled on a stunned Bianca. "After we get rid of this douche bag here, I'll be back. Probably for the reception. Because I'm a good friend like that." Without waiting for a reply, she turned and marched out of the building.

Alex shot the gathering of people an apologetic look for the interruption. Then he hauled the handcuffed vampire to his feet and followed Lacy out to the parking lot. It was dark enough now that he didn't have to worry, but when they'd arrived, he'd been forced to make a mad dash into the church to avoid the sunlight. His shoulders had smoked for a good five minutes after that, requiring him to hide in one of the men's bathroom stalls until he was presentable.

As he followed Lacy out to the car, for once, he wasn't eyeing her backside. His stomach felt like lead. Shapiro knew who he was. Who knew what else the psychotic vampire had on him? The investigation had suddenly gotten much more dangerous. This attack had proved that with certainty.

When Lacy reached the car, she turned to look at him with a questioning expression. "So what now? Are we going after this Shapiro guy?"

"*We* aren't doing anything," he snapped in reply. "This has gotten way too dangerous for you." He gave an annoyed snort. "No. It's always been too dangerous for you. I've just been thinking with my dick and not my brain."

"I've been perfectly fine," she retorted. "You worry too much."

"He doesn't worry enough," the hostage vampire said, interjecting into their conversation. "Shapiro will kill you both before this night is finished. You're dead, girl. Dead."

Alex slammed the vampire against the side of the car. "Shut up!" His attention quickly returned to Lacy. "Though he's partially right. I didn't worry enough. It was insane for me to involve you in any of this. That first morning..." He shook his head sadly. "I should have walked away that morning. I should have gotten an annulment. It would have been safer that way."

"There is no safety in Shapiro's town." The vampire cut into the conversation once again, this time with a malicious sneer. "Only death awaits those who come here and don't abide by his rules."

Alex growled in the back of his throat and snatched out the stake he had hidden in the breast pocket of his suit jacket. With a quick flick of his wrist, he staked the vampire, relishing in the silence that followed.

"I thought you wanted to interrogate him," Lacy said in an injured tone.

Alex shook his head. "No. I just couldn't stake him in front of all those witnesses."

"Oh," she said softly.

He watched her for a moment in silence, feeling guilty at the way her eyes were downcast to the pavement at her feet. Her expression was one of emotional torment. He forced his guilt down and looked away from her. "I'm going after Shapiro. You should go back inside."

"I don't want to go back in there," she argued. "I'll be too worried about you."

"Lacy, you're not coming with me," he said firmly.

She blanched at the harsh tone of his voice. "You... You'll come back. Right?"

He stared at her hands, watching her wring them anxiously. "I'm not coming back." He finally looked at her face and hated himself for the panicked look he saw in her eyes.

"Then I'll leave and wait for you at the hotel. I can't go back in there by myself. I don't even like those people anyway."

"Lacy," he said solemnly, "I'm not coming back at all. I think it's time we came to our senses and ended this. The longer we wait, the harder it will be."

"I...I don't understand," she whispered.

"My life is too dangerous. I don't want to be responsible if something happens to you. You don't belong with me. You belong in there, with them."

"I belong with the people who hurt me? I belong with the man who cheated on me and the friend he cheated with?"

"I don't know, Lacy," he said with a weary sigh. "I just know you don't belong with me."

"I love you," she said softly, her voice quavering.

"This isn't love. It's lust, and really good sex, but it isn't love."

A tear tracked silently down her cheek following his statement.

Realizing how that had sounded, Alex attempted to be kinder. "Lacy, you know I'm right about this. You might think you have feelings for me now, but think about your future."

"I am thinking about my future," she cried desperately. "I want my future to be with you! I want to move to Green Bay and snuggle under a blanket to stay warm when we're buried under four feet of snow. After we're done with your case here, I want to see your home. I want to make love in every room of it like we did here."

Trying not to let his expression show how much he would regret not getting to do all those things, Alex said, "Short term, that's all great. For a few years, we might even be happy. Eventually, you are going to want children. I can't give you that. You'll want someone to grow old with, and I can't give you that either. I'm always going to be this. I can't age. I can't reproduce. I can't change."

"I don't want you to change," Lacy said with a whimper. Her tears fell freely now. "I don't care about any of those things. I don't want that stuff. I want *you*."

"I'm not going to rob you of a full, happy life, of a family." He waved a hand at his chest. "This life isn't fulfilling. It's cold, and it's lonely."

"It doesn't have to be."

He shook his head miserably. "Our marriage was nothing more than a drunken mistake. Please don't take that as a slight to you as an individual. You're a charming and beautiful woman, but this just wasn't meant to be. We never would have done this had we been sober."

"At the beginning of our first night together, I wasn't nearly as drunk as you." She spat the words angrily at him and swiped at the tears on her cheeks. "I made a conscious decision to approach you. You weren't like all the other pushy and grabby men at the bar. You looked so sad and lonesome. You looked like you needed me."

"You meant for this to happen?" Alex asked in outrage. Had he really been a victim of her coy manipulation all this time? Had he played into the hand she'd dealt him without ever stopping to question any of it?

"No!" Lacy's eyes narrowed into a glare, contrasting with her tears. "I didn't mean for all of this to happen. You just... You looked so vulnerable that night. I think I fell in love with you there on the spot." Sniffling, she rubbed her nose with the back of her hand. "I just wanted to get to know you. That's all. I wanted to talk for a little bit to take some of the sadness out of your eyes. All the other crazy stuff happened after I started drinking, once we were both drunk."

Her confession made him feel even crueler, but his decision never wavered. "I'm sorry, Lacy," he said with regret. "I'm honored that you chose me that night, but it doesn't change anything. We're from different worlds." Reaching out, he took one of her hands in his and kissed her palm. "I'm sorry I hurt you." His eyes held hers for what he feared was the last time. "You'll get over me soon enough. You'll find a good man, one who deserves you. Then you'll see how right I am about this." Letting go of her hand, he climbed behind the wheel of his car.

Her eyes widened and alarm filled their blue depths. "Grimm, don't do this."

Avoiding her gaze, he started the engine. "Go back inside, Lacy."

"Grimm, don't leave me with these people. I need you."

"I don't need you," he said dully, his heart sinking at the pain he knew this statement would cause.

She flinched away from him as if slapped. "Grimm, please." As he put the car in reverse and backed out of his parking space, she yelled after him. "Grimm!" Swallowing back tears, she hollered out his name. "Alex! Alex, please!"

Her desperate sobs were the last things he heard, and they echoed in his ears once he was well out of hearing range.

Chapter Twelve

Alex spent the entire drive to Shapiro's not planning, but feeling guilty over the tears he'd caused Lacy to shed. He'd been a monster to her, and he knew it. As he sat outside in the parking lot of the Caribbean Chateau, he envisioned her now, probably face down on their bed, her shoulders trembling with sobs.

He hoped she'd come to hate him soon. Hatred was easier to deal with than despair. He would know. He'd been substituting one for the other for years. "Damn it," he said with a growl, and slammed his fist into the steering wheel. He who had spent centuries putting walls around his heart and avoiding emotional ties could think of nothing more than pulling Lacy into his arms and kissing away her tears. Memories of her filled him—her smile, her scent, her everything.

With a snarl of frustration, he climbed out of his car and slammed the door violently behind him. Without so much as the slightest plan, he marched toward the hotel.

This wasn't like him at all. He always went in with a plan. He went in with a backup plan. Sometimes, he went in with a backup to the backup plan. Now, he was so concerned with a life he couldn't have that he was going in half-assed. "Fuck it," he said darkly. Nothing he'd been doing recently had been much like him. Why stop now?

Marching in the front door like a vigilante cowboy, Alex pulled his gun from the waistband of his slacks. Clicking the safety off, he strode through the lobby with the gun held loosely at his side.

When he reached the reception desk, he raised his weapon

up to point at the clerk's nose. "I want to see Shapiro Langston. Take me to him, or I will pull this trigger and end you."

The desk clerk bared her fangs and gave a ferocious hiss.
"Your gun does not frighten me. Do your worst."

His lip twitched in amusement, and he glanced over his
shoulder into the lobby. "It would do horrible things to the
tasty humans, though. Take me to see Shapiro now, or I will
give you a newsworthy bloodbath in your lobby. I know your
boss would hate it if attention was drawn to his establishment and people started associating it with murder."

Arrogance filled her features. Straightening her shoulders, she spoke to him in a superior tone. "Men like you don't
kill humans. You don't have the balls for it."

His eyebrows arched in amusement, and he returned to
his original tactic. "True. I won't kill the innocent bystanders
dumb enough to stay here. I wouldn't be so certain about the
gun's effects on you, though." His grin turned malicious.
"Wooden bullets."

He watched as the confidence oozed out of her. She
cursed under her breath, glaring daggers at him. Biting her
lip, she flicked her eyes down to the weapon. After a moment
in which she must have seen no escape from her situation,
she nodded toward a long corridor. "Follow me."

Casting one last hateful look over her shoulder, she led
him farther into the hotel. She moved away from the humans and their cheery din, Alex hot on her heels. As they
approached a meeting room at the end of the long hallway,
she led him inside.

At the back of the office was a doorway that appeared to
be a closet. She opened this door and stepped back to reveal
a passageway down to a dark and foreboding basement.
"The boss will kill you," she said with spite. "You are dead."

Alex stared down the stairs into the gloom beyond. "With
the luck I've been having, you might be right." He nudged
her into the stairwell ahead of him. "You'd better hope not,
because if Shapiro kills me, you're next for showing me
where to find him."

Her eyes widened at the apparent truth of his statement.
She walked hesitantly as he forced her down the steps, her
heels dragging against the ground. "He will kill us. No one is
allowed down here. Mr. Langston conducts his private busi-

ness down here. He does not like to be disturbed."

As they hit the bottom of the darkened stairway, lights suddenly flared to life, illuminating the basement. "Let him down, Olivia." The voice belonged to a well-groomed business man who stood in the center of the open space beyond the steps. His expression was calm and unconcerned. He stood patiently, his hands clasped serenely behind his back.

"But, Mr. Langston..." The woman with Alex took an uncertain step forward. "He has a gun. It—"

Shapiro cut her off with a snap of his fingers. "Olivia, leave us." His voice oozed tranquility and smoothness, and he arched a dark eyebrow in her direction.

"But—"

"I said go!" The façade cracked only momentarily before Shapiro cleared his throat and continued in a much calmer tone. "Mr. Grimm and I have a meeting. We've been awaiting his arrival."

Olivia nodded consent, her eyes downcast. She turned and started back up the steps. As she passed Alex, she shot him a nasty sneer. "You're dead."

Alex ignored her. He was more concerned with the fact that Shapiro had been waiting for him. Once again, the other vampire was one step ahead. It was an ugly reminder that Alex had bitten off more than he could chew with this case.

"Well, come forward." The words were spoken invitingly, as if Alex was a guest being asked to join Shapiro for lunch. "You forced your way into my establishment by holding Olivia at gunpoint. Don't be shy now."

Cautiously, Alex stepped farther into the room. He had to maneuver around a few packing crates to fully view the entirety of the large, open space. Once his visual field was clear, he screeched to a halt with an involuntary gasp.

Across the room, Lacy stood bound in front of a bulky vampire. Her wrists were tied behind her back and a gag had been stuffed into her mouth. When she saw him, she attempted to scream, but the sound was smothered by the cloth between her lips. She struggled against the vampire, trying to force her way free. She hollered and fought, doing everything she could to make his job more difficult.

The vampire growled and clubbed his forearm roughly against the side of her head.

Lacy gave a squeak, sounding like an injured animal. Her eyelashes fluttered rapidly as she battled with unconsciousness. She managed to keep her eyes open, if half-lidded, but Alex saw the fight drain out of her.

With a growl, he took a menacing step forward. As he did, his eyes landed on his sister. Regina's eyes were downcast and full of remorse. While these men had manhandled his wife, she'd been unable to do anything without blowing her cover. Alex's eyes quickly swept back to Shapiro, his hands fisting with rage.

"What did you think was going to happen?" Shapiro asked conversationally. "I'm the most connected man in all of Vegas, and you left your tasty human alone. Of course I was going to scoop her up. It all but ensured my victory." He shook his head in mock disappointment. "Such a careless thing to do with a woman you supposedly care about."

Alex looked closer at Lacy and clenched his fists at the sight of the blood that trailed down her neck, disappearing into the top of her dress. "You bastard." He spat the words at Shapiro with outrage. "How dare you touch her?"

Shapiro chuckled, placing a hand to his chest. "My, my. Such rage." He cocked his head to the side and offered up a mocking expression. "Almost as angry as I was when I discovered my best blood retriever was dead, killed by a traitorous vampire who hunts down his own kind. All to protect the blood bags no less."

"Marcus deserved what he got." Realizing his attitude was not going to secure Lacy's safe release, Alex attempted another tactic. "She is innocent in all of this. She had nothing to do with Marcus or his death."

"It's true." Shapiro played lazily with the sleeve of his suit jacket, as if the outcome of the situation mattered little to him. This nonchalance made Alex more edgy than he cared to admit. "Her only crime is being associated with you." An evil grin crossed his lips, and Alex knew something bad was about to come from them. "There are others in your small circle that have done far worse." His head tilted in Regina's direction, his ice blue eyes locking onto hers. "Isn't that right? Sis?" As her eyes widened with astonishment, he nodded to the vampire behind her. "Grab her."

The vampire obediently stepped forward and wrapped a

meaty arm around Regina's throat, yanking her back against his chest. "I've been waiting all day to play with you, kitten."

Regina hissed, baring fangs as she struggled against his grip.

"You're a feisty little thing, aren't you?" the vampire asked. "I'm going to enjoy punishing you. Very much."

Alex immediately moved toward his sister to assist her, but Shapiro's next comment stopped him in his tracks.

"Which do you want?"

The words sent a cold chill down Alex's spine. They seemed to reverberate through his entire being, freezing him from the inside as they swept along. *Which do you want?* He knew exactly where Shapiro was going with this, but he still questioned it all the same. "What?"

Shapiro's expression turned downright malicious. "Which one do you want? If you leave now and never return to my city, I will permit you to leave with one of the women in your life still alive."

As if catching on to the cruel joke, the vampires brought Lacy and Regina to stand next to each other. "Which do you spare?" Shapiro asked in a low, curious voice. "Your sister? Or your fuck buddy?"

Alex's stomach turned. Hearing it aloud was more appalling than the mere thought. Shapiro was honestly going to make him decide between Lacy and Regina. "What kind of sick offering is this?"

"One much too generous for such a thorn in my side." The words were spat with anger, but Shapiro quickly smoothed out his expression to be neutral once again. He waved a hand at Lacy, then at Regina. "So which is it? Spare one, and the other dies now. In front of you."

Alex trained his horrified eyes on the women in question. His options weren't really options at all. How could he be expected to choose between Lacy and Regina? He couldn't. He wouldn't.

Lacy's eyes were wild with horror. Her shoulders were rising and falling rapidly, as if she was on the verge of hyperventilating. He knew by the way she quivered with terror that she assumed she would be the sacrifice.

Alex slid his eyes to Regina. She had gone silent and still, her eyes boring into his. Her eyes were so intense that he had to look away.

"I take your silence as a rejection to my offer? You'd rather see them both dead if it means solving your little case?" Shapiro asked.

"You're killing innocent people. I can't just walk away from that."

Shapiro sighed. "You inconvenience me." He motioned to the two vampires holding Lacy and Regina. "Kill them. Then kill him."

Before the vampires could react, Regina twisted in her captor's grip. In one swift movement, she brought her elbow back into his nose, then dropped to a crouch. Yanking a stake from her knee-high boot, she lunged upward with a vicious growl. She wielded the stake like a knife and slashed it toward the vampire's cheek, tearing a large gash in his face.

The vampire howled in pain while his companion stared fixated in uncertainty. He shifted his feet as if contemplating coming to his friend's aid, but instead tightened his grip on Lacy.

When the vampire she'd attacked instinctively reached up to his face to assess the damage, Regina slammed the stake violently into his chest. She gave a ferocious holler and twisted the stake to assure that it punctured his heart.

As his ally turned to dust, the second vampire changed his tactics. Looking slightly panicked, he dropped Lacy to the floor and spun to face Regina with his fists raised.

She was gripping the stake tightly in her palm, her breath escaping in short, angry pants. "Come on, big boy. You guys liked knocking around a defenseless human girl. Let's see how fun you think it is when someone has the ability to fight back."

Alex's chest swelled with pride, but he didn't have a chance to watch any further, because two vampires converged on him from the shadows. He barely managed to duck and roll out of the way as they both swung at him with simultaneous attacks. Before he even got to his feet, he had one of his stakes in his hand.

One of the vampires was blatantly young where the supernatural was concerned, young enough that he was still arrogant about his new powers. He might be stronger than all of his old human buddies, but he was not stronger than a much older and more experienced vampire. He had obviously trained in martial arts as a mortal and thought this would give him an advantage. He came at Alex with loud hollers and fancy footwork, not realizing these skills couldn't stand up to a few hundred years of experience.

When the vampire spun around with a heel kick, Alex blocked him with a forearm. The impact hurt, but it didn't do nearly enough damage for the effort put in. Alex then slammed his elbow down on the vampire's knee. He heard bone shatter a moment before the vampire screamed in agony. "Hurts like a bitch, doesn't it?"

Before the vampire could respond, Alex slammed his stake deep into his chest. He spun to face the second vampire in one smooth motion, his hand still gripped tightly to his weapon.

The second man was holding back, being more cautious. He and Alex stared at each other in silence, each eyeing up their opponent.

It was Shapiro's voice that finally cut through the quiet. "You can go home, Joshua."

"But sir..." The vampire's eyes widened with surprise. "Don't you think—"

"I do not need you to fight my battles," Shapiro said as he slid out of his suit jacket. He folded it neatly before setting it carefully aside. "I wouldn't have gotten where I am today if I didn't know how to get my hands dirty."

Joshua hesitated, uncertainty plain on his face. "Are you sure?"

Shapiro whirled on him, his eyes bulging with the anger that suddenly filled their depths. "Go home! I do not need you here. Do not disobey me!"

With one last uncertain look at the man in charge, Joshua disappeared up the steps toward the main floor of the hotel.

Alex only watched him out of the corner of his eye. His main focus was Shapiro, and he refused to take his attention off of the intimidating crime lord for even a second. It took a powerful vampire to be secure in the outcome of a fight such as this, especially when lives were on the line. One might think Shapiro an egomaniac to put himself at such a disadvantage, but Alex thought he was just that old, just that good at being an enforcer. "I'm guessing you didn't get rid of him so we could peacefully discuss the shutdown of your operation?"

Shapiro smiled, his expression amused and at ease. "Not at all." His grin widened, becoming almost demonic. "Joshua can be a bit squeamish. I didn't want him whimpering and whining at the sight of what I plan to do to your human once I kill you." He glanced at Lacy over his shoulder. "The only question is, do I use her and then drain her? Or do I keep her around as my sex slave and blood donor?"

Alex tensed, but refused to react any more than that. He knew Shapiro was playing at his emotions, trying to get him to do something careless. "I would prefer it if you stopped forcing me to listen to you talk and simply fought."

Shapiro gave a gentlemanly nod. "That does appear to be our only option." He moved a step closer, his body still appearing relaxed and calm. "I'll have you know, if she survives, I'll give your sister the same courtesy as the human. One can never have too many sexual pets at their disposal."

Rage built inside Alex, his fury boiling just under his skin, but he kept himself composed. He would die before letting this man get his hands on either Lacy or Regina.

An instant after his comment about Regina, Shapiro sprang. There was no tell, no indication that he was about to move. He was just suddenly crossing the room with the speed of something far from human. One moment he was still, the next he was at Alex's throat. His hand clawed around Alex's windpipe, his fingers digging into flesh. He yanked backwards roughly in an attempt to rip Alex's throat out.

Alex barely managed to free himself enough to keep his esophagus intact. Even so, he could feel the damage and knew there would be deep, angry welts along his throat. He felt blood trickling down his neck, and the gouges left behind burned. Still, he laughed. "You didn't think it was going to be that easy, did you?"

Shapiro skated back, his eyes filling with caution. "Just testing the waters."

Seeing the hesitation in the other man when he didn't receive immediate results, Alex launched an attack of his own. He might not ever get another opportunity to have the upper hand. He wasn't about to waste it. He hit Shapiro with a right hook, trying to merely daze his opponent to slow him down.

As Shapiro reeled from the hit, Alex gave him a shot to the jaw with his left fist. Then he swung back around with the right, catching the other vampire in the temple. He went back and forth. Right. Left. Right. Left. Somewhere along the way, he'd lost his stake, but he didn't linger on that. He put his entire focus on his fists. He punched until his knuckles were caked in the other man's blood. The silly manicure Lacy had talked him into getting was definitely ruined.

Grabbing a stake he'd shoved into his suit jacket pocket, Alex swung it upward at Shapiro's chest, attempting to finish things off quickly.

The other vampire threw himself backward with super-human speed, flying into a row of cabinets along the wall. "You filthy traitor." Spitting blood and what appeared to be a tooth to the ground at his feet, Shapiro inched slowly back toward Alex. "You are a disgrace to vampires everywhere, fraternizing with human filth. They aren't meant for companionship. They are food. Entertainment. Nothing more."

"They're more than just food to me," Alex said softly. "*She's* more to me."

"You're willing to die to protect dinner."

Alex glanced ever so quickly in Lacy's direction. With relief, he saw that Regina had managed to untangle herself from the others. She yanked the gag out of Lacy's mouth and began working on the knots that bound her wrists behind her back. He didn't allow himself any more than that quick glance at the two women before returning his eyes to Shapiro. "I guess I am."

"Foolish!" Shapiro's accusation was made while he rolled up the sleeves of his dress shirt, as if really preparing for the dirty work. "But so be it." He lunged at Alex, moving in a blur.

Alex managed to bring his foot up into Shapiro's chest, halting his attack. In the same motion, he took a swing at the vampire's head.

Using speed Alex only hoped to one day possess, Shapiro ducked under Alex's blow. Pulling a stake from within his shirt sleeve, he jammed it roughly into Alex's chest. It appeared no mistake that he'd missed the heart. Shapiro was toying with him. Instead of taking a killing blow, he'd punctured a lung with the jagged wood.

Alex jerked back and went to gasp, but he couldn't pull

air properly into his lungs. Though it wasn't necessary for a vampire to breathe, most still did, purely out of habit. The injury to his lung wouldn't kill him, but it threw him off, distracted him. It was an ingrained reaction to panic when one couldn't breathe. Vampires were not immune to this.

Though he struggled, Alex quickly got his fear under control, but the constant pain every time he involuntarily attempted to draw in air was disruptive to his concentration. He was no longer able to even think about getting on the offensive. It was a battle simply to block the other vampire's punches and kicks. He was slowly being worn down. His arms ached from the blows being rained down upon them, and his reactions were becoming slower.

Alex took a kick to the ribs and cringed as he felt a crack resonate through his chest cavity. Shapiro had broken a rib, putting additional pressure on his chest. Between that and the lung, it was nearly impossible to think around the pain.

With Alex distracted, Shapiro went in for the kill. No longer did he use coy words or toy with his victim. His intentions now were murder. His aim was perfect, and the stake would have ended Alex had Lacy not jumped onto his back.

She caused Shapiro to weave on his feet, the stake going wide of its target to slide along Alex's arm instead of imbedding into his heart. "Stop it!" She screamed the words, her voice shrill. "Don't hurt him!"

With a ferocious snarl, Shapiro whirled to the side, trying to knock Lacy off of his back. When that didn't work, he reached an arm over his head, grabbed her by the back of her dress, and threw her away from him.

Lacy went flying into the cement wall headfirst. Alex heard a sickening crack, like an egg being dropped on a sidewalk. He watched her eyes go dull as she slid to the floor. True panic seized him at the sight of her crumpled body. That sound had been her skull colliding with the wall.

He suddenly cared about nothing else but getting to Lacy. He didn't care about the case. He didn't care about revenge. He didn't care about Shapiro. Without conscious thought, he grabbed his gun from the waistband of his slacks. For a moment, he just stared at it.

When Alex lifted his gaze to Shapiro's, he knew he didn't care about his precious, hard to find wooden bullets. He raised the gun even with Shapiro's heart.

Shapiro laughed in amusement and spread his arms wide, giving Alex an easier shot. "Go ahead. Take a free shot with your useless human weapon. That pathetic thing won't even slow me down." He shook his head as if in disappointment. "You're so blinded by them and their contraptions that you forget who you are dealing with. Monsters of the night cannot be stopped by man's steel."

While Shapiro filled the air with meaningless chatter, Alex pulled the trigger, wanting to get past the one obstacle between himself and Lacy. He watched with grim satisfaction as the bullet penetrated the other vampire's chest.

Shapiro's mouth opened as if he was about to speak, but then his eyes widened in surprise. He clutched his chest and looked down at it in horror.

"Wooden bullets," Alex said a moment before Shapiro disintegrated into dust. He rushed forward, not even taking the time to feel satisfaction at his victory. He'd officially taken down the group responsible for so much death, but at what cost? His stomach full of dread, Alex raced to Lacy's side and dropped to his knees by her head.

Regina was already there, having staked the vampire she'd been battling with after she'd freed Lacy. She ran her fingers gently along the back of Lacy's skull. Her mouth was pinched with worry. "Her skull is fractured," she said grimly. "In multiple places."

Her eyes locked with his, and Alex could see the gravity she was trying to convey.

"I think..." She sighed and removed one of her hands from behind Lacy's head to grip his forearm. When her fingers slid along his skin, she glanced down at them as if surprised to find them covered in so much blood. Her wide eyes returned to his. "She's dying." The words were whispered, as if saying them quietly might negate their truthfulness. "I'm afraid that even if we get her to a hospital right away, she still won't make it."

"She's dying," Alex repeated in a dull voice. His eyes lowered to Lacy's pale face, and he traced the curve of her lower lip. His body felt cold and empty, his heart frozen. His Lacy was dying.

"She doesn't have to," Regina said in a low, breathless

tone. "Turn her."

Alex's gaze whipped to hers. "Are you insane?" He scooted away from them on the floor, trying to put some distance between himself and that suggestion. "I could never do that to her."

"Do what?" Regina asked almost frantically. She tried to smooth some of Lacy's hair back from her face, but only managed to mat it with blood. "Save her? She's dying, Alex. If you don't do something really soon, you're going to lose her forever."

He was fairly certain he'd already done that when he left her on the sidewalk outside that church. "I can't rob her of a fulfilling life. I can't take away her options. She could become a mother. I'm not going to murder her future child. We'll take her to a hospital. They'll save her." Crawling back to them, he cautiously lifted Lacy into his arms and climbed carefully to his feet. She gave a soft whimper of pain, but thankfully, never woke.

He took a step toward the staircase, but Regina put a restraining hand on his arm. "If you take her up those steps, she's as good as dead." She gave a frustrated holler and threw her hands into the air. "Alex, there is no baby! There is no future. If you don't turn her, she dies. There won't be a growing old. There won't be a Lacy. That girl will be gone. The only thing you'll be cheating by turning her is death."

Alex froze. His legs couldn't move him any farther toward the steps, yet his brain couldn't accept the truth of Regina's statement. They stood in near silence, the only sound the occasional drip as Lacy's blood hit the floor.

"Alex..." Regina's whispered voice broke into his panicked thoughts. "Do you love her?"

The answer came easily. He didn't even need to look at Lacy's angelic face to find the answer. Love had never been the problem. "Yes." He whispered the word, and it trembled past his lips.

"Then turn her."

His eyes held his sister's for a moment. Then he lowered Lacy back to the floor. "I just hope I'm not too late."

"If her heart is still beating, it's not too late."

His hand went to Lacy's throat, and time seemed to stand still as he searched for signs of life. After what felt like far too long, he found the dull thump of her pulse. "She's alive," he said with relief. "Barely."

"There won't be a need to drain her," Regina advised. "She's lost enough blood on her own."

He nodded, more anxious than he'd ever felt in his entire life.

As if sensing his unease, Regina gave his arm a reassuring squeeze before pulling a knife from a sheath strapped to her boot. "Here. Before she bleeds to death."

Alex took the knife, but held her wrist to get her full attention. "Thank you. If you wouldn't have talked me into this..." He shook his head. "Thank you for being here with me. I wouldn't want it to be anyone else."

Regina rolled her eyes and shook her arm free of his grasp. "Just do it already before I gag," she said with a little smile.

Rolling his eyes in return, Alex sliced a large cut into his wrist. Carefully, he held it over Lacy's mouth while Regina held the girl's head still.

"The wrist," Regina grumbled. "How cliché."

Ignoring her, he set to work at feeding Lacy his blood. He moved slowly, watching each drop as it dribbled past her lips.

It was a few minutes of this before Regina spoke. "Alex?" she asked softly.

He glanced up from Lacy almost in surprise. He'd been so focused on his task, he'd nearly forgotten he wasn't alone. "Yeah?"

"You hesitated."

"What?" he asked, brows furrowing in confusion.

"When Shapiro told you to choose between Lacy and me, you hesitated."

Guilt welled up inside him. "I'm sorry, Regina." He paused, trying to think of a way to explain himself without injuring her feelings. "I know you're my flesh and blood, but I'm crazy about her."

Regina punched him roughly in the arm. "I'm not mad that you thought about choosing her! I'm mad that you didn't!"

He blinked at her in bafflement. "Come again?"

"I'm a vampire," she said in way of explanation, her tone exasperated. "I can take care of myself!" She motioned toward Lacy's still form. "She's human! She's fragile and gentle. She needs you. I don't. It'd be embarrassing being rescued by my little brother. I'd rather fight my own battles." She stuck her tongue out at him before continuing. "Besides, for some unknown reason, that girl seems to love the hell out of you. She should know she comes first in your life."

Alex squeezed his wrist, dripping more blood down Lacy's throat. "I won't have to look after her once we're done here," he said almost bitterly. "She won't be human anymore."

Regina shot him a look of annoyance. "Alex!" She gave a huff of aggravation. "That shouldn't matter! You should always look out for her! If you love her, she should always come first."

Alex looked down at Lacy and brushed her hair back from her face. "She will."

After this declaration, both he and Regina fell silent. They sat this way for what felt like hours. They watched wordlessly while Lacy's body went through the change. Alex held her when spasms wracked her body. It had been a long time since he'd witnessed the change work its way through someone. It had never been pleasant, but watching it happen to Lacy was almost more than he could bear.

Just when he thought she could take no more, her body went still. His eyes lifted to Regina's to find them wide and expectant. They held each other's gazes for a moment before both lowered their eyes back to Lacy. Just as Alex did, his wife's eyelashes fluttered open.

"Alex?" she asked weakly.

His hand reached out to cover one of hers. "I'm here. I'm here, Lacy, and I'm never leaving you again."

With speed she hadn't possessed a few hours before, Lacy lunged to a sitting position and wrapped her arms around his neck for a tight hug.

Caught off guard, Alex quickly braced one hand against the ground so he didn't topple down onto her. With his other arm, he returned the embrace. Closing his eyes, he allowed himself to be fully consumed by her presence. He'd thought he would never hold her again, which made this moment almost heavenly.

"I was so worried about you," she said against the side of his neck.

Alex pulled back in astonishment. "Worried about *me*?

Lacy, you *died*." He shook his head. "You don't have to worry about me."

"You're my husband. It's my job to worry about you. Doesn't matter that you're the toughest, bad ass vampire I've ever met."

With a laugh, he pressed his lips briefly to hers before resting his forehead against hers. "I love you, Lacy Grimm. Don't you ever forget that."

"I love you too, Alex Grimm." She stroked her fingers along his jaw before pulling back slightly to give him inquisitive eyes. "I do have one question, though..."

His eyes searched her face. "What? I'll tell you anything you want to know."

She surprised him with her next comment. "Do we still have time to make the reception?"

***

A few hours later, Alex found himself somewhere he thought he'd never be, at Bianca and Bernard's wedding reception.

After she'd regained consciousness, all Lacy could talk about was making the reception. She hadn't asked how she was alive or any questions about her new lifestyle. Once she'd gotten the confirmation that she could safely be around humans for a couple of hours without wanting to rip their throats out, she couldn't be deterred.

So here he was, seated at a table with two strange men while Lacy and Regina tore up the dance floor. He watched Lacy twirl and pump her fists in the air, gyrating to the beat that hammered through the speaker system.

She whooped and cheered, looking like she didn't have a care in the world. And maybe, being the zany woman she was, Lacy didn't.

A male guest was inching closer and closer to her, obviously working up the nerve to dance with her.

The men sharing the table with him whistled and pointed in amusement. One nodded to Alex with a grin. "Our buddy is so about to hook up with that bridesmaid! She is so drunk."

The two men bumped their fists together, the second one saying, "This is why I love weddings."

Alex's gaze slid lazily to Lacy. She was now dancing with the man, swinging her hips almost suggestively in time with the music. He could see how a bystander might think she was drunk, but she was just in a silly mood. She hadn't had a drop to drink this evening...at least not of alcohol.

Turning back to the men, Alex tapped his fingers against the tabletop, his expression full of amusement. "That bridesmaid would be my wife."

The two men exchanged a look of embarrassment. The one on the left coughed uncomfortably into his hand while the other said, "Man, I'm sorry. I didn't realize..." He glanced at the dance floor and grimaced at what he saw. "It doesn't bother you that she dances with other men like that?"

As the music changed from fast and pulsing to slow and romantic, Alex sat down his glass of vodka. "My wife's a dick magnet," he explained in amusement, his thoughts going to the song that had played in his car the night she introduced him to the world of oral sex.

With that, he calmly walked away. He made his way confidently to the dance floor, tapped the strange man dancing with his wife on the shoulder, and said, "May I cut in?" The man frowned with displeasure, so Alex felt the need to explain. "I'd like a turn with my wife, if you don't mind."

The man's eyes widened in horror and the hand he had on Lacy's hip instantly snapped back. "Sure. No problem, dude."

Lacy shot the man a wide, friendly grin. "Thanks, Jeff."

With an embarrassed nod, he slunk away.

A snicker sounded behind them, and Alex glanced over to see Regina.

"I think I'll go comfort Jeff on his loss," she said as she made her way past them toward the seating area. She eyed the table Alex had come from. "And perhaps his cute friends as well." She patted Alex on the shoulder. "Jeff's blond friend will be giving me a ride home...tomorrow." She winked. "Don't wait up."

"Regina..." Alex's voice was a growl of warning as she sauntered away. Out of the corner of his eye, he saw Lacy watching him expectantly. Forgetting all about Regina, he turned to his wife. With a grin and a roll of his eyes, he held a hand out to her and asked, "Can I have this dance?"

"Sure." Lacy's arms slipped around his neck, and she stepped in against him. "Poor Jeff."

"Poor Jeff?" he asked in disbelief.

"You went all scary vampire on him," she said with a purr. "Though I found it sexy, the look you gave him practically made him piss himself."

Alex snorted. "It did not."

"Come here, you big, bad vampire." Lacy pulled him toward her and leaned her head on his shoulder. They stayed like this for a while, swaying silently to the music.

Though he didn't speak, Alex's mind was a whir of activity. He hadn't said much to Lacy since she'd opened her eyes as a vampire. She'd wanted a shower to clean the blood from the back of her head. Then Regina had helped Lacy with her hair and makeup, the two of them going as far as washing Lacy's dress in the sink to get out the worst of the stains. It wasn't great, but it was passable. The girls had figured the guests already knew she was in a tussle at the church. They would just have to deal with the dirt and other various stains.

Immediately after getting cleaned up, they'd rushed here, where the girls were partying up a storm on the dance floor. He was glad to see them getting along, but he was relieved to finally have Lacy all to himself. He had some apologizing to do. Tightening his arms around her, he whispered into her hair, "I'm sorry."

She tensed in his arms. He thought she might ignore him, but she finally tilted her head back to look up with unshed tears in her eyes. "For what?"

He didn't even know where to begin. "For everything," he admitted. He moved a hand from her waist to brush away a tear that escaped her eyelashes onto her cheek. "Including making you cry right now."

Lacy bit her lower lip and appeared to be trying to keep herself from full-out tears.

Alex looked away from her, surprised at the strong emotions that arose inside of him at the sight of tears sparkling in her eyes. He had to swallow down a lump in his throat before he could look at her again. "I never meant to hurt you." His voice was quiet, regretful. "I only left because I was trying to protect you." He tightened his left arm around her waist, holding her closer to his chest. "My life is dangerous. I didn't want to be constantly putting you in harm's way."

"I know," she said softly. She hesitated, then said, "While she helped wash bone fragments out of my hair, Regina told me part of your hang up about turning me...the whole baby issue."

He cringed at the mental image of her picking pieces of her skull from her hair. He was suddenly glad the girls had locked themselves in the bathroom to get dolled up. Had he seen pieces of Lacy's chipped skull in the bathroom drain, he just might have lost his sanity.

"Grimm," she said firmly, bringing his attention back to her. "I told you before that all I wanted is you. I never mentioned that I couldn't have children. I was born with messed up ovaries." She shrugged. "That was another reason Bernard chose Bianca over me. She could give him a child."

Every piece of Alex wept with relief. He hadn't changed anything about her future. She was never destined to have children. Nor did she have any close family. She had no ties to miss. She was perfect for him. "Bernard was an idiot." Releasing her waist, he grabbed her face in both hands and kissed her, reveling in her soft mumble of response.

Lacy's body softened against his, her curves fitting perfectly against him.

Pulling back, he forced her to look deep into his eyes. "I love you, Sunshine," he said, using her nickname for the first time. "I am going to spend the rest of eternity making these past couple days up to you. If you'll still have me, that is." Upon waking, she'd confessed her love for him, but now she'd had time to think on things. She'd had time to think on how hurtful he'd been. He was so worried she would come to her senses and leave him. Surely he deserved as much for the way he'd hurt her.

Her arms wrapped tightly around his neck and she pressed her lips to his. He could feel her arms trembling with emotion. "Of course I'll have you. You are my life now. There isn't any other way I'd have it."

"Good," he whispered into her neck. "Then I'm guessing it wouldn't be out of line for me to ask you to marry me."

Lacy giggled and pulled back slightly so she could look at him. "We're already married, Grimm."

He rolled his eyes in response. "Fine. I suppose technically it would be considered renewing our vows. I don't remember how you looked when we got married, and I want to see you in a big, beautiful gown. I want you to be the center of attention." He huffed, knowing he was putting too much importance on this. Regardless, he couldn't help himself. "Lacy Grimm, will you marry me? Again? Will you re-marry me?" His eyebrows drew together in a frown. "I'm not getting down on one knee in front of all these people." On her amused expression, he sighed. "Fine." He dropped to his knee. "Will you marry me already?"

Laughing, she pulled him to his feet. "Yes! Just get up!" She wrapped her arms around his waist in a tight hug. "I forgive you. Stop torturing yourself."

"So you'll move to Green Bay with me?"

Lacy nodded, a smile of pure pleasure spreading across her face. "I will. But I want my own closet."

"I'll give you two." He slid a hand seductively along her hip. "I believe I also remember you mentioning having sex in every room of my house. Are you still up for that?"

"Yes." She arched an eyebrow and wiggled against him. "I can tell you are, too."

Desire raced through him, hot and all-consuming. "How about we blow off the rest of this reception and head back to our room?"

"Sounds wonderful." Lacy nuzzled his neck, her breath warm against his throat. "I can't wait to sink my teeth into you."

Epilogue

"You're going to be busy..." Regina was prattling in Alex's ear, but he was having a hard time concentrating on her. "Very busy, I'm assuming. That is why, as part of my wedding gift to you, I am going to track down the last vampire involved with this nasty business. Joshua, you said? Yes? Blond, curly hair. Stands about six-four. Caucasian."

"Uh-huh." Alex was barely listening to her. His attention was all for his beautiful bride. "Vampire. Fangs."

"It is my duty as the maid of honor to make sure you guys have a fun, stress-free honeymoon."

"I think you should concentrate on your other bridesmaid duties right now," he said with amusement, finally turning to look at her.

Regina blinked at him in confusion. "What's that? I thought I'd covered everything fairly well. I—"

Spinning her to face Lacy, Alex pushed Regina toward a group of overly eager guests. Out of pure instinct, she caught the bouquet that came flying her way. As soon as her fingers closed around the flowers, her eyes widened with horror.

Laughing, Alex crossed the dance floor and pulled Lacy into his arms. "Death and violence we're okay with, but imply we'll be next to get married and you'll see real terror in a vampire's eyes."

Lacy giggled and wrapped her arms around his neck. "Oh, I don't know," she teased. "You seem comfortable with the married life."

"Psh." Alex scoffed at this. "You should have seen me that first morning you showed up in my life. I was sweating bullets."

"Glad to see you've gotten over your fears." She nuzzled against his throat, pressing her lips to his jugular. "Though there is something I hope stays the same this time around."

Alex pulled back to look at her with surprise. "I can't imagine what. The hangovers. The memory loss. The death. The heartache..."

"I was thinking more along the lines of consummating our marriage in all kinds of crazy places." Her lip curved up wickedly. "There is a limo outside that we have for a few more hours. Might be a nice place to start."

Their eyes met, and nothing else needed to be said. Grabbing her hand, Alex pulled her in the direction of the parking lot.

As they hurried past her, Regina called out after them, waving her bouquet frantically in the air. "Wait! Where are you going? We still have to cut the cake!"

Lacy waved to her over her shoulder. "We'll be back. Stall for us for a little bit, please. We have.. something important to attend to."

Alex swung her up into his arms and kicked the hall door open. "Do we ever."

About the Author

Melissa lives near Pittsburgh, Pennsylvania with her husband, Jeremy, and her son, Marshall Frost. Her favorite genre to write is Paranormal Romance.

Melissa attended London School of Journalism where she received her certificate in Novel Writing in 2011. She writes a monthly short story column titled *Frequent Flyer* for a government newsletter.

www.ingramcontent.com/pod-product-compliance
Lightning Source LLC
Chambersburg PA
CBHW030533130626
46552CB00006B/2240